MW01530751

Billionaire's Daughter

Making of an Heiress

Bea M. Jaffrey

Disclaimer

This is a work of fiction. Names, characters, businesses, places, events and incidents are either the products of the author's imagination or used in a fictitious manner. Any resemblance to actual persons, living or dead, or actual events is purely coincidental.

Copyright © 2017 Bea M. Jaffrey

All rights reserved. No part of this book may be reprinted, reproduced or utilized in any form or by any electronic, mechanical, or other means, now known or hereafter invented, including photocopying and recording, or in any information storage or retrieval system, without permission in writing from the author.

ISBN: 197920196X
ISBN-13: 978-1979201964
Edition 1:11

Dr. Bea's web site: live-best-life.com

To Anna

1

GENEVA, SWITZERLAND

The old man sat by the window, looking over Lake Geneva. In his hands, he held a letter he'd just read but couldn't quite comprehend what it said, so he read it again:

Dear Mr. Duponte,

My name is Anna Andersson and I believe that I am your daughter. This might come as a shock to you but let me explain. My mother, Cecilia Andersson, met you 26 years ago at the Cannes film festival. According to my aunt Birgitta, my mom's sister, you were dating that summer and my mom became pregnant with me. She moved back to Sweden shortly after and the following year I was born.

My mom never spoke of you. She seemed very upset whenever I asked her questions about my father. My birth certificate states "Father Unknown."

Unfortunately, my mom passed away two months ago. Though she knew she had terminal cancer and only a limited time to live, she insisted on not disclosing your identity to me.

At her funeral, my aunt told me your name and the name of your company in Geneva, so I found you on the internet and after much consideration, decided to write you this letter. I don't know what happened between the two of you but I'm curious about my father and would like to meet you in the near future. You have my details here below, you can either email me or call me. I live in Gothenburg, on the west coast, so if you ever come to Sweden, please stop by. If you don't want to see me, that's okay, I understand.

Sincerely,

Anna

Henri Duponte put the letter on his lap, taking a moment to digest the news.

"Goddammit!" he said out loud. "Clotilde!" he shouted to his secretary next door. "Can you come in here?"

Clotilde, a blonde lady in her late 50s, immaculately dressed in a gray conservative skirt suit and black Ferragamo pumps, came in running. "Yes, Monsieur Duponte? What can I do for you?"

"Call Mike, I want to see him straight away."

"Yes sir," she replied and disappeared back to her room. She was clever enough not to ask questions, only follow the orders when the big boss called.

Mike, a gray-haired man in his early 50s entered the office ten minutes later wearing a black suit, white shirt and a slim black tie. One could mistakenly take him for Tommy Lee Jones in the movie *Men in Black*. A hard-edged personality paired with muscular physique.

"You wanted to see me sir?" he asked in a deep guttural voice.

"Yes," Mr. Duponte answered, "thank you for

coming on such short notice, much appreciated."

"No problem sir. What can I do for you?"

"I want you on the first flight tomorrow morning to Sweden. You are going to Gothenburg. Ask Clotilde to arrange your flight and a hotel."

"Sweden?" Mike asked cautiously. He had been to Stockholm but never to Gothenburg.

"Yes," Mr. Duponte answered, his words coming out a bit irate. "I want you to find out everything you can about a young woman called Anna Andersson. She is 25 years old. Here is her cell number and email address." He paused then added, "Here is her home address." He gave Mike a piece of paper and an empty envelope with the sender's address label on.

"I want you to follow her 24/7. Take pictures and report to me directly, at least twice a day. And keep your distance. I don't want her to know she is being followed. Don't mention this to anyone."

"Yes, of course Sir," Mike answered. I'm not a fool, he thought but said nothing.

"Good," his boss said, his mood lifting. "Any questions?"

"Hmm," Mike was not sure if it was appropriate to ask but ventured anyway, "For how long would you like me to follow Miss Andersson, sir?"

"That depends on what you can find out about her. Few days should be sufficient. I will let you know," he said while looking out the window.

"Of course sir, may I leave now?"

"Yes, go speak to Clotilde. She will arrange everything. Ask her to come see me if she has any questions."

"Yes sir," Mike said politely. "I will be on my way now." He turned and left the room swiftly.

2

GOTHENBURG, SWEDEN

Gothenburg, or Göteborg in Swedish, the second largest city after Stockholm, situated at the west coast of Sweden is a windy place. During summer months, the Nordic sea breeze can be felt through the Götaland region. Anna, on her way back from work, drove her Mini Cooper across the Älvsborg Bridge. The high suspension bridge connects the city north and south and is almost one kilometer long. Suddenly, a strong gust of wind hit her car causing the vehicle to sway into the other lane. She gripped the wheel frantically.

"Shit!" she shouted.

Crossing the tall bridge always scared her. The other option would be to take the tunnel under the Göta River but that was even more terrifying. She felt claustrophobic in the long tunnel, especially during rush hour when the traffic was slow. She felt trapped in her small car, imagining the worst disasters that could happen; from fire in the tunnel to the roof collapsing on her, causing river water to flood the tunnel, drowning her slowly. Oh no, she would rather take the windy bridge and hold on to the steering wheel anxiously. There was also the old bascule bridge in the center, the Götaälvbro, but that was a nightmare to cross as far as Anna was concerned. Last time she tried that bridge, it opened up for the boat traffic below so she was stuck for 20 minutes on top of it while several ships passed underneath.

Note to self: look for new job in the city, avoid the island of Hisingen.

Once she was safe on the mainland, Anna texted her best friend Elin.

"Fika?"

Elin responded with a thumb up emoji and a smiley. "Where are you?" she added.

"Will be there in 10," Anna answered.

Fika (you say fee-ka) is a Swedish word for afternoon tea though it can take place anytime during the day. It's a coffee break with pastries, cookies or sandwiches. Some people have tea instead of coffee and the children get saft (a kind of lemonade) or juice to drink. Fika can be both a noun and a verb in the Swedish language. Swedes drink a lot of coffee, they are on the top list of worldwide coffee consumption. Most socializing events take place around fika. It's also the number one first date choice for couples; much less informal than dinner or drinks.

Anna pulled into a parking space, lucky to find one just outside of Elin's house, which in the center of Gothenburg, felt like winning a lottery. When she got to the door, she let herself in by pressing the security code on the main entrance door and ran three floors up to greet her friend.

"Hej," she said to Elin. "What's up? Have you been home all day?"

"Yeah, just got up," Elin answered lazily still wearing her pajamas though it was 4:30 in the afternoon. "Stefan is in Stockholm so nothing much happening here."

Stefan was Elin's sugar daddy. He was 30 years older than Elin but this didn't bother her at all. He had money and was generous, that was all that mattered to her. He also paid for her flat, including all the monthly bills, grocery shopping and spending money. They travelled together on his private jet to places like London, Paris, Rome and Monte Carlo. He bought her expensive gifts. Last Christmas she got a Rolex watch and on her birthday he presented her with a Cartier Love bracelet with diamonds.

The apartment belonged to his company so if the relationship ended, Elin could find herself on the street. Nevertheless, she was happy with the arrangement. Coming from a poor background she valued financial security in whatever form it came to her. The downside was that Stefan was married with no intention of getting a divorce. According to him, the company belonged to his wife as well, so divorce was impossible. Anna felt Stefan was using Elin, that she could do so much better without him, but who was she to judge? As Elin rightly pointed out, she was getting extremely well paid for something that most women give away for free. Besides that, all men were either losers or cheaters, or both, as Elin put it. Anna's latest boyfriend Christer was no exception. They had been dating for six months when Anna introduced him to her friend at work – Ewa. Within a week Christer dumped Anna and hooked up with Ewa. His excuse was that Anna was too busy with her sick mother so it wouldn't have worked anyhow, but she knew that she wasn't good enough for him.

"Karma is a bitch," said Elin at the time. "Wait and see," she added.

Anna was very hurt by the betrayal. She couldn't face Ewa at work, often running off to the washroom to cry in solitude. How could a friend do this to her? Who needs enemies when you have friends like this? A few months later, Christer got caught while cheating on Ewa with a coworker.

"I told you so," said Elin. "You see, my Stefan is not so bad after all," she added. The fact that she would spend most of her time alone, waiting for his calls and longing for him like crazy, did bother her but she didn't want to come across as clingy, knowing Stefan would end the relationship if she did. He made that clear last December when Elin wanted to spend Christmas and New Year's eve with him. "Out of the question," he blurted. She cried for two days. On the third day a huge parcel arrived with extravagant Christmas gifts from Stefan and life was good again.

"You want to see my new Louboutins?" Elin said, her voice shrill with excitement. "They arrived yesterday from Paris."

"Sure," Anna answered. Another pair of platform shoes that no one could wear for more than one hour. Besides that, they cost a fortune. Anna's monthly salary could buy either one pair of Louboutins or one small Chanel bag. That excluded paying her rent or having money for other things. She could not afford the same expensive items that Elin bought. She was still paying off her beloved second-hand Mini Cooper, thus money was tight. One day she would buy a brand new car, straight from the factory, especially made for her just like the Volvos on the assembly line, tagged on the windshields with their new owner's names. Yes, one day her dream will come true and no amount of shoes, bags or exclusive beauty treatments would measure up to that, her brand new car.

Despite Elin's superficiality and her extravagant spending habits, Anna adored her friend. They had known each other since kindergarten. Inside the materialistic Elin was a heart of gold that few people knew about. Anna appreciated their friendship immensely. She knew she could trust Elin. Besides that, Elin had a good sense of humor and was fun to hang out with. She was also very beautiful. Tall and slender with long blond hair that fell across large blue eyes, she looked like a younger and more natural version of Victoria Silvstedt, the Barbie looking Swedish model and television personality. Elin had smaller breasts and less hair than Victoria, but she was still stunning. Since she hooked up with her sugar daddy, she had a nose job, liposuction on her thighs, lip fillers and botox treatments, which Anna thought was totally unnecessary. Now she wanted a boob job, just like Victoria did.

Elin spent several hours a week on self-maintenance. She did facials, manicures, pedicures, hair treatments, hair extensions, eyelash extensions, waxing, laser hair removals, eyebrow shaping and tinting, massages, sun beds etc. It seemed to be full time work for her as almost every day she had a treatment booked somewhere. She didn't go to the gym though, only to yoga classes, because she hated the sweaty, smelly guys drooling after her at the gym. Wherever Elin went, men tried to pursue her. This could also be due to the fact that Elin never left the house without full makeup. She always looked like a model ready for a photo shoot so of course men noticed her. When the two of them went out together, no one paid any attention to Anna; all eyes were on Elin. This didn't bother Anna at all as she considered their friendship to be very special. As far as Anna was concerned, Elin could get away with murder.

She would never forget that fateful day when Elin stood up to Lars, the class bully, in third grade, slapping him on the face for calling Anna a "homeless Gypsy." She was always the odd one looking, an easy target for the bullies. Since that day their friendship grew closer, through thick and thin, through pain, tears and laughter, they were always there for each other, no matter what.

Anna watched as Elin tried on the black patent heels with red soles, parading across her living room.

"What do you think? Should I keep these? Can you take some pictures for me so I can post them on Instagram?"

"Sure," Anna answered. "Just pull up your pants so I can take some close-ups."

Anna had grown used to taking pictures of Elin who had over 300,000 followers on Instagram. She would buy expensive stuff, try it on and photograph everything, then send at least half of the items back, or sell them on the Internet. Of course, her followers didn't know that, they believed that Elin was super rich and super famous.

"Have you heard anything from Geneva? Did he get your letter?" Elin asked Anna.

"No, nothing yet. The tracking shows that he got the letter yesterday but so far no news."

"I wonder why your mom hated him so much that she told you he was dead and never wanted to talk about him. What did he do to her?"

"I don't know," said Anna. "Must have been something serious for her to keep him out of my life. I still feel guilty for writing to him. She would have been so mad at me if she knew."

"Well, your mom is dead now and you have the right to know. Especially now after finding out his name and how loaded he is. Can you imagine? Your dad is one of the richest men in Europe. He is a billionaire for God's sake. Embrace that. You better get used to being rich girl. Kudos to you!"

Anna was not so sure about all that. What if Henri Duponte was not her father after all? Did she make a fool of herself sending him the letter? And if indeed he was her father, maybe he wouldn't like her? Thoughts bounced around in her head. She worried he didn't care if she was his daughter. Compared to Elin, Anna was a plain young woman. Her shoulder-length mousy brown hair was usually tied in a pony tail. Her hazel-brown eyes were unlike her mom's and her aunt's light blue ones – a typical Swedish eye color. Some kids in school even asked her if she was adopted because she didn't look like her mother. She would invent lies and tell them that her father was a prince from a far away country and that one day he would come to whisk her away on his private jet. So much for fairy tales.

In her teenage years, Anna felt insecure. Her skin was not as clear as she wished it to be; breaking out frequently, especially around her period. She didn't use as much make up as Elin, though she tried to hide the random acne spots as much as possible, without going overboard on the concealer. Although Anna was a little heavier than Elin, they shared the same size so she could borrow her clothes for special occasions. Anna's clothes and shoes purchased at cheap stores like H&M or Zara, were plain compared to Elin's. She could never afford the higher quality dresses, the extravagant bags like Elin's or the haircuts from leading salons. Instead, her mom used to cut her hair, before she got sick. Anna's eyes teared up when thinking of her mom.

For the past two years Anna had been taking care of her sick mother; taking her to the doctors and driving her to the hospital for chemo therapy, radiation and physiotherapy. She also bought countless meds and made sure they were taken at the right time. Besides that, there was grocery shopping, cooking, cleaning and running errands, while working part time at the Volvo factory's account department.

By the end Anna was exhausted so when her mother finally passed away it felt like a huge relief as well as great sadness.

The funeral was extremely emotional to Anna. Seeing her mother's coffin in front of the altar made it so real. She finally understood that her mother was gone forever, that she would never talk to her again, never ask how her day had been or call her on the phone. She will not be there when Anna gets married or when her first child is born. These thoughts were unbearable to her, she couldn't stop crying. She didn't care that she looked a mess in front of all these people in the church paying their respects. She didn't care about all the words that the priest said during the ceremony. If there was a God in that church that day, how was it possible that he took away her only parent and made her an orphan at 25 years-old? Her mom was a good person, why did he take her away? Why?

Anna's aunt Birgitta tried to console her, and it was there, at the wake reception, where her aunt dropped the bomb regarding Anna's father and looking him up. She gave Anna his name and the name of his company in Switzerland. Apparently, she had promised her sister to never disclose his name to Anna, but under the unfortunate circumstances, she decided otherwise.

She believed that Anna had the right to know who her father was. She found him on the internet and almost choked on her coffee when she realized that Anna's father was a wealthy man. This was too good to be true. Her niece could inherit a fortune; it was her birthright after all.

"So should I keep them or not? What do you think?"

"Why don't you try on the other 15 pairs that you already have in your closet and then decide?" Anna said with a cheeky smile.

They both laughed out loud.

"Coffee?"

Mike landed at the Landvetter airport just before noon. There were no direct flights from Geneva to Gothenburg so he had to take a connecting flight in Brussels. What a hassle, he thought. Mike was a tough guy but he hated airplanes. He didn't trust the pilots, maybe because he had seen too much in his life, too many human errors. He was a military veteran who served in the Kuwait Gulf War under general Schwarzkopf, then got recruited by the CIA who sent him to Stockholm. After a few months in Sweden he was transferred to the U.S. Mission in Geneva.

At that time he didn't know much about Europe. As so many fellow Americans, he confused Sweden with Switzerland. He learned that Stockholm is the capital of Sweden, a country north of Europe. Together with Norway and Denmark, Sweden is part of Scandinavia, the former land of Vikings. Switzerland on the other hand is located in the heart of Europe, bordering to Germany, France, Italy, Liechtenstein and Austria.

Switzerland is tiny compared to Sweden as its area is 41,000 square kilometers compared to Sweden's 447,000. So Sweden is the size of California and Switzerland slightly bigger than Maryland. Both countries have almost equal population of 10 million people which is less than the population of New York City.

In Sweden people speak Swedish and in Switzerland there is no language called *Swiss* but the four languages which are German, French, Italian and Romansh – the official languages of the Swiss Confederation. Bern is the capital of Switzerland. Bern and Zurich are located in the north-east, the German part. Geneva and Lausanne, both located in the western part by the Lake Geneva, or Lake Leman as it is called locally, are French spoken.

The south of Switzerland with the city of Lugano and the canton of Ticino belong to the Italian part of the country. The fourth language Romansh, originating from Latin, is spoken in the canton of Grisons located next to Ticino in the south of Switzerland.

3

GENEVA, SWITZERLAND

When Mike moved to Geneva he didn't speak a word of French. The city is home to many international organizations. Among others, the United Nations and the Red Cross are located here. Several big corporations have their headquarters in Geneva. It is estimated that 50% of inhabitants are foreigners so the city is truly international, making it possible to get around with English language only.

Mike's lack of French was not a big problem as most of his colleagues at the U.S. mission didn't know the language either. French is difficult to learn for an Anglophone. Mike took evening classes after work but quickly got frustrated. What a stupid language, he thought. It doesn't sound the way you write it as there are many silent letters so often two different words sound the same which was very confusing to him. He came to the conclusion that he was too old to learn it properly and after a few months of mental torture he finally gave up.

Mike's career with the U.S. mission ended abruptly when despite all warnings from his bosses, he married a Russian woman. The sayings "Once a CIA agent, always a CIA agent" or "You can never leave the Agency" are not true. They fired him the day after he got married. Frankly, he didn't have a choice.

Mike met Elena shortly after moving from Stockholm to Geneva. On Friday nights, a group of guys from the mission would have drinks after work. It was one of these nights that Elena happened to spill her Bloody Mary on Mike's shirt. At first he was pissed, thinking his shirt was ruined, but she was so sweet and humble when apologizing to him that Mike took pity on her. Although he was long-distance dating a Swedish girl named Mia at the time, and not interested in new relationships, Elena was persistent in pursuing him.

One thing led to another, as it often does, and within a matter of days Elena was calling Mike, inviting him to the movies or asking for help with leaking kitchen taps. When Mia arrived to spend the weekend with Mike in Geneva, Elena showed up at the front door with a bottle of wine, wearing a sexy red dress and very high stiletto heels. Mia was furious with Mike. At first she thought Elena was a hooker who rang the wrong door bell, but soon Mike explained that they actually knew each other quite well.

This was a very awkward situation. Finally, he asked Elena to leave. No amount of explanations could convince the fuming Mia that nothing had happened between Mike and Elena. The next day Mia left for Stockholm, never to be seen again. Mike tried to call her to no avail. So bye, bye Mia, hello Elena.

With Mia out of the way, Elena's plan to snare Mike was promptly put into action. Within a few weeks she moved in with Mike because her lease ran out and couldn't be renewed. Then her visa had run out so the only option for her to stay in Switzerland was to get married. Mike was not ready for marriage, at least not to Elena. He was still missing Mia and daydreaming about telling Elena how incompatible they were, hoping they would part as friends. The day he finally summoned his courage to have "the talk," Elena announced that she was pregnant.

Abortion was out of question as suddenly, the never going to church or praying Elena, told him she was very religious and absolutely wanted to keep the baby. How was she pregnant? Mike asked her. Did she forget to take her pill? What happened? She didn't know, she said. Must be God's will, she added.

They got married on a Tuesday afternoon in a civil ceremony at the Geneva City Hall's registry office – the Mairie. Only a couple of Mike's buddies attended the nuptials. The four of them had dinner and drinks at a local pub afterwards.

The next day Mike went to work and immediately got fired. He had been warned by his bosses not to get involved with anyone from the Eastern Bloc but he didn't listen. He believed that he did the right thing, as the honorable man he was, he took his responsibility. This was during the Cold War when the military and political tension between the United States and the Soviet Union was high. Any personal connections with the "enemy" was considered treachery.

With a baby on the way and no income between them, Mike was desperate to find work, any work. One day he saw an ad for a bodyguard. "Must speak English. Must travel," it said. He was lucky to get the job. Soon he discovered that the person he was hired to protect was Henri Duponte. He would travel with Mr. Duponte on his private jet and follow every step his boss took. In reality he carried the bags and ran errands for his boss but it didn't bother him too much as the pay was good and after each trip he had a few days off from work. The Swiss employee protection system took care of that. He also had free health insurance for him and Elena.

It was during one of these trips that Elena informed Mike by phone about her miscarriage. She said she had lost the baby that morning but that she was fine. He was overwhelmed by the news. Though the pregnancy was not planned, Mike got used to the idea of becoming a father. He was looking forward to raising the baby, even hoping it would be a son. He envisioned them playing football together, going hiking in the summer and skiing in the winter. He was disappointed that Elena lost the baby. Wait a minute, he thought. How do I know there was a baby? Maybe she lied to me. Maybe all she wanted was to get married so she could stay in Switzerland. He got even more suspicious when Elena seemed to not care about the miscarriage. Her lack of emotions baffled him. Who is this woman? How could I marry someone that I don't know?

A couple of weeks later Elena told Mike that her cousin from Moscow would come to visit. Could Mike find him a job? Just for three months she said. So now he was not only married to a Russian woman, he was supposed to find work for her family members as well. What a drag.

One day Mike arrived home from work to be greeted by Elena's cousin Boris, a Popeye the Sailor lookalike. Boris, a big guy with a huge torso and heavy tattooed muscled arms, looked like he had spent the last few months pumping iron. Matter of fact, Mike later found out that is exactly what Boris had done, at the Moscow prison.

"Hello, I'm Boris," he said in a heavy Russian accent reaching his right arm out to Mike. "How do you do?"

Mike shook his hand, looking him straight in the eyes. He was not sure if he liked the guy or not. Elena seemed happy to have him there.

"Honey," she said to Mike. "Boris will sleep on the sofa, okay?"

What was he suppose to say? Not okay? Go to a hotel? He said nothing as Elena was already in the kitchen preparing dinner. At least she cooked when Boris was around so something positive came out of it.

When dinner was on the table, Boris came in with a bottle of Russian vodka.

"We must celebrate," he said. "This is my first

time abroad. Elena, where are the glasses?"

Elena put three standard glasses down, the ones that you would drink water from and not strong alcohol.

"This is the way we do it in Russia," she said.

Boris poured the vodka almost to the brim of each glass.

"Na zdarovje! To your health," he said lifting up his glass.

Mike couldn't believe his eyes when Boris gulped the full glass of vodka in one go. WTF! He gasped and cursed in his mind. Elena took only a sip from her glass, promptly putting it down while Mike was still standing there in disbelief.

"Drink Mike! Drink!" Boris encouraged Mike. "A real man knows how to drink."

A few hours later the two men were both asleep on the same sofa, totally drunk.

Mike wasn't able to find work for Boris. He didn't try that hard because he didn't want to be seen together with the man. It was enough that the guy stayed with them, ate their food, and drank alcohol each night that Mike paid for. Elena seemed happy to have her cousin around. She cooked every night and didn't complain much.

It was a canceled business trip that would change Mike's life forever. He was due to follow Mr. Duponte to New York when his boss changed his mind at the last minute. As it was late, Mike decided not to call home in case Elena and Boris were already asleep. It was almost midnight when Mike opened his front door. The lights were off in the living room but he could hear faint noises coming from the bedroom.

He opened the bedroom door to see Elena and Boris naked in bed together. She was on top of him, riding him frantically, her back turned towards the door. Boris was moaning, with his eyes closed, looking like he was going to climax shortly. Mike just stood there frozen. His mind raced uncontrollably. He got furious. All the time he had believed that Boris was Elena's cousin and now this? What a fool he had been!

In a split second, Mike raced toward the bed, his face red and snarled in anger. He grabbed Elena by her hair and pulled her up from Boris.

"You whore!" he shouted. "Get out of my house! Now! You and your lover, get out!"

Boris looked perplexed then jumped from the bed, shaking as he grabbed his belongings. Mike dragged the naked, screaming Elena to the front door. Boris sprung forward to help her but Mike would have none of it. He opened the door, pushed Elena out and turned to Boris and punched him in the face. Boris tried to punch back but he was too drunk and Mike was faster than him, avoiding the punch by ducking down. He pushed Boris outside and quickly locked the door.

He could hear Elena crying outside and Boris banging on the door. A neighbor must have called the police because within 15 minutes they were outside Mike's apartment.

"Police! Open up! Ouvrez! Police!" they shouted in French.

Mike looked through the peephole to see what was going on. He saw two police officers, a couple of next door neighbors and a naked Elena hiding behind

Boris' hairy back. The policeman was still banging on the door.

"Keep calm," Mike said to himself. He went looking for Boris' duffle bag. "You son of a bitch, you are going back to Russia!" he screamed while gathering Boris' clothes and shoes, throwing them inside the bag. Next, he went to the kitchen and got few garbage bags to collect Elena's clothes. He was fuming with rage while stuffing the bags with clothes and shoes. The policeman was still banging on the door, screaming "Ouvrez! Police!"

"Yes, I'm coming!" Mike shouted at them. After piling the bags in front of the door, he unlocked it, trying to push the clothes out of the apartment. The policeman forcefully shoved open the door, grabbed Mike and pressed him forcefully to the wall, pulling his arms behind his back and handcuffing him.

"Let me explain," said Mike calmly to the policeman, though he was boiling inside. "This is my apartment and I found this guy here in bed with my wife. They need to leave. I don't want them here." The policeman, still holding on to Mike from behind, said something in French to his colleague. Elena and Boris were already inside the apartment. She went to the bedroom to get dressed; meanwhile Boris was sitting on the sofa, half naked, with a baffled look on his face.

Mike tried to stay calm. The last thing he needed in his life was to get arrested for domestic violence. With his hands behind his back, face pressed to the wall and a cop on his back, there was nothing he could do.

The second policeman came back with Elena, now dressed in her bathrobe. She collected her clothes that were thrown in the garbage bags. Elena cried, cursing Mike, playing the wronged victim. She marched off with her clothes toward the bedroom, the second policeman trailing after her. Within minutes another patrol car arrived. This time with a female police officer.

The female police officer questioned Elena in the bedroom. After a few minutes, which seemed like an eternity to Mike, she came back to talk to the others. Mike didn't understand a word of what they said but finally one of the policemen spoke English to Mike.

"You will have to come with us to the police station for questioning," he said.

"But this is my apartment," Mike responded. "You can't leave them here, they should not be here!"

"Your wife says that she lives here so she has the right to stay. She also says that her friend was invited by both of you and that you were okay with him living here."

"That was before he screwed my wife!" Mike shouted out, losing his cool. "She told me he was her cousin, not her lover!"

"I understand that," said the policeman, "But you need to come to the police station now to sort this out."

There was no other way of getting out of this mess than going to the station. I may as well cooperate with the cops or they will make more trouble for me, Mike thought.

Mike spent the night in an isolation cell. The next

morning he was interrogated by the police. They told him that Elena and Boris had pressed charges against him and that he could not return to his apartment alone. Someone would go with him to collect his things. He would have to find another place to live, at least until the trial, and was ordered to stay away from her or be arrested.

"What trial?" Mike asked. "I didn't do anything wrong," he added.

"Well, your wife thinks differently so the judge will have to decide."

Upon his release from jail the following day, Mike went straight to the office to see his boss. Henri Duponte was not happy to hear the news.

"You must understand Mike that I can't keep you on if this thing goes to trial. I just can't. Is there any way that you can negotiate a settlement with your wife?"

"I don't know sir," Mike responded anxiously. "I wouldn't know where to start. I was ordered to stay away from her."

"You need a good lawyer and a new place to stay. Let me make some phone calls and get back to you," Mr. Duponte said to Mike not quite believing what he just offered him to do. Well, the guy got in trouble after I cancelled my trip so I am partially to blame for his misfortune, he thought.

A week later Mike and Elena signed an agreement in front of his boss' lawyer stating that she was to keep Mike's apartment, also his life savings, and to receive monthly alimony for the next 10 years, unless she married before that time. Mike knew that would never happen; she would milk him to the last drop. In exchange, she and Boris dropped their charges against him. Mike was a free man, although a very poor free man.

"It's only money," Henri Duponte said to him. "You will make more, don't worry. See the positives here; you got rid of your cheating wife. It was worth every penny."

Mike was not so sure about that. It's easy for rich people to say "it's only money" but for us who have to work so hard to get any, it's a different ball game. But his boss was right about the freedom aspect of it. It felt great to finally be free. At that moment Mike knew he would never get married again, and most importantly, he would never trust another woman as long as he lived.

4

GOTHENBURG, SWEDEN

To stay incognito in the home of Volvo cars, Mike rented a black Volvo XC90. He imagined that most people in this city would drive the locally made vehicle. He was partially wrong as the streets were lined with other makes like Volkswagens, Audis, BMWs, Toyotas, Mercedes, Fords and Saabs. Only 10% of Swedes drive a Volvo. The Gothenburg factory employs 14,000 people out of the half a million that live in the city.

He checked in at the Posten Hotel, a modern hotel close to the train station, located in the old post office building. The hotel was charming, originally built in 1925. The lobby was busy, allowing him some anonymity. Old habits from the CIA days die hard.

Once in his room, he unpacked the few things he brought and went straight to work. He had already done some research about Anna on the internet. Her name was so common in Sweden that over 200 Anna Anderssons popped up in Gothenburg alone and a total of 9,000 in the country. He couldn't find her on Facebook or any other social media but Sweden's transparency laws made it possible to find her on the tax payers list. She was registered at the address Mr. Duponte gave him, living alone in an apartment of 60 square meters. The web site also told him that she was driving a Mini Cooper. What he wanted to see was a picture but unfortunately there wasn't any. So he chose to go to the apartment block where she lived and wait for her.

Mike stood in front of Anna's apartment building. A quick look at the names in the entrance told him that her flat was on the fifth floor. The entrance door, however, was locked with a code so he couldn't get in. Sooner or later, he knew someone would pass through the door so he had to be patient and wait. After few minutes an old lady came out allowing him the opportunity to sneak inside. On the fifth floor there were three apartments, Anna's was the first one from the lift.

He carefully opened the mail slot on the door to see if he could hear anything.. There was no one there, but staying inside the building would look suspicious, so he went outside to wait in his car. Several hours passed with not much happening; no Mini and no Anna to be seen. Then suddenly, just after 8 p.m., a blue Mini Cooper pulled into the parking place opposite the building. A young woman with a shoulder length pony tail, jeans and a blazer, got out of the car and headed to the main entrance.

"Bingo!" Mike said to himself. He took out his camera and started taking pictures.

In the days that followed, Mike learned that Anna worked part time at the Volvo factory's account department. She kept mostly to herself, had lunch at work and meeting her model-like friend in the afternoons. She shopped for groceries at the local ICA market.

There was not much to report to Geneva. The girl was obviously an introvert, with no boyfriend, no one else in her life, except the hot Barbie model. Mike wondered if the two women could be in a relationship with all the frequent visits. On few occasions he followed them outside of the apartment, but didn't notice any hand holding or loving looks. Mostly they laughed together. He also noticed that the Barbie doll drew plenty of attention to her. Men stared and women were jealous of her beauty. She seemed confident for her age, compared to Anna who seemed a little insecure. Mike could tell straight away that Anna's posture and behavior were different from her friend's. She didn't know that she was beautiful in her own right.

Henri Duponte looked at the photographs Mike sent. His heart pounded and he felt adrenaline running through his body. Life was strange, he thought. Out of the blue, at a time in his life when nothing could surprise him anymore, suddenly this happened. The possibility that he could be a father to this young lady in the photos was not that big as he always made sure to use protection when having sex, but there was something about her face that reminded him of his late mother. There was a remarkable resemblance that he couldn't ignore. The only way to be sure was to take a DNA test, which meant a call to his doctor.

"Mike?" Henri called Sweden. "Can you get me a hair from Anna? I need it for a DNA test. But the problem is that you need to pluck it from her head as a lose hair strand will not be enough. We need the root of the hair."

"I'll try," Mike said, wondering how he would pull this one off. He would try to get close to her at the ICA check-out, but how would he pull out a hair without her feeling it? And without blowing his cover? Besides that, her hair was always tied in a pony tail. How do you pull a hair out of that? He needed to call his old friend at the CIA.

Mike's friend said that any hair with the root still attached to it was good for a DNA test. Try to get into her bathroom and find hair in her brush. Look for the tiny root at the end of the strand. Take several hairs to be sure.

"Copy that," Mike said.

When Anna went to work the next morning, Mike went to her apartment dressed as a plumber in a blue boiler suit. He let himself in by picking the lock with two hair pins, something he had learned long time ago at the CIA. Jiggling the pins into place, it took him only ten seconds to get inside. Great, he thought, Swedish locks are so easy to pick. People here are not used to putting extra locks on doors.

Not much crime here I guess.

He found her brush in the bathroom and luckily there were a few hair strands with the roots still attached. He slid them into a small zip lock bag. "Mission accomplished," he said with a smug smile on his face.

5

GENEVA, SWITZERLAND

Henri Duponte was very pleased with Mike's Swedish trip. The guy delivered again, he thought. The benefit of employing an ex-agent was greater than the trouble the man had caused him some years ago. Henri helped him then and Mike never forgot it staying loyal to his boss all these years. So yes, Henri was happy. Now he needed to know if the girl was his.

At the age of 76, Henri Duponte was still a good looking man; a Harrison Ford lookalike with hazel brown eyes and gray hair. Henri had never missed a day of work in his entire life. Just like his father, Henri Duponte senior, he was a driven businessman, and one of the wealthiest people in Switzerland. Though his father was rich and powerful, Henri was proud to have built his own empire without his father's help. In his mind, he was a self-made man, though people always believed that he inherited the family company and the Duponte fortune. The truth was, though, his brother David, 10 years his senior and his father's favorite, the "Duponte crown prince," inherited most of the family's businesses. When their parents died in a car accident, some 50 years ago, Henri was left at David's mercy. He was only 26 years-old at the time, and David was 36, and married with three children.

In their father's will, David, who was also made executor of the will was put in charge of everything, the whole family empire. Henri's anger at his father grew and it showed in his actions. He hated his father for not trusting him more, for not acknowledging his capability to run the company on equal terms with David. He believed that his competence was on par with David's, that he could even do better than his brother. But it was not to be, he was not good enough in his father's eyes. He felt like an outcast.

Henri worked 18 months alongside David but with each day he realized that he wanted to be his own boss. David treated him fairly, so that was not the problem. It was the other people; the employees, the business friends, and the extended family members, who saw him as the little brother of the boss, instead of paying him due respect as they should have.

Finally, he'd enough of playing second fiddle, so with the help of his father's lawyer and a private banker, he decided to open his own company.

Geneva is a small city there everyone who matters knows each other. Fifty years ago it was even more important than today to know the right people. From bankers to lawyers, to the city's politicians, Henri's father was well connected. These connections came in handy for Henri, especially knowing who owed his father a favor and who could be bought for money. When an older family member wanted to sell a building in the old town of Geneva, Henri took his chance. He borrowed the money from the bank at a low interest rate and no deposit. The private banker trusted Henri's decision since the building had exclusive apartments with high-priced rentals.

The revenues from the building were relatively good so shortly after, Henri could afford to buy another at a very cheap price. This one was a dilapidated, older house, also in the old city of Geneva. It needed to be renovated so Henri hired cheap labor in the neighboring France, a practice that city officials were not happy about because they wanted to keep these jobs for the Swiss workers. With some bribes in the right places, he managed to finish the renovation quickly with no complaints from the city council.

The building, modern on the inside, yet still keeping the outside old charm, became the talk of the town. People lined up to rent apartments from Henri despite the high rent. His business grew quickly. Shortly he expanded to other cities and then countries. He opened offices in the south of France, then Paris, London, New York, Los Angeles and Dubai. From apartment blocks to office buildings, from hotels to skyscrapers, his real estate empire blossomed. The day he opened his own bank, he knew he had made it. Henri was on a roll, life was good.

The early 90s recession hit Switzerland as well as the United States. Henri kept a low profile, thus sailing smoothly through difficult times. David, on the other hand, couldn't cope with the pressures. Within a year his company went bankrupt, which created a huge buzz in the local community. David was devastated. When Henri reached out to him offering help, David told him to go to hell. He would cease his pain and feelings of shame with whiskey. While drunk and desperate, he became violent toward his wife who threatened to leave him. One night when she was asleep, he took his gun and shot himself in the head.

Henri found out about his brother's suicide on the morning news while driving to work. He immediately turned around and drove to the cemetery there both his parents rested in the Duponte family grave. While kneeling in front of their tomb, his head buried in his hands, he cried like he never cried before. These were the first tears he'd shed since he was a child.

The feelings of guilt overwhelmed Henri as he felt responsible for David's death. He believed he had failed his brother. He could have helped him financially if David would have allowed him to. His brother was too proud to beg for money. He would rather kill himself than admit to his younger brother that he was broke.

Henri lashed out over his father's gravesite.

"Oh father, why didn't you believe in me?" he cried out facing the tomb. "Why didn't you love me as much as you loved David? What did I do to you that you mistrusted me? If it wasn't for you, David would be alive today."

Henri was back at the same cemetery two weeks later to bury his brother next to his parents. He envisioned his own tomb in front of him. What will my obituary say? he thought. How will people remember me? Will anyone miss me when I'm gone?

At the time of his brother's death, Henri was married to Mathilda, a Swiss German woman, his former secretary. They had a son called Maxence. Besides taking care of her son, Mathilda, 10 years younger than Henri, kept to herself. She didn't like to travel or to socialize with Henri's business friends. She also had many health issues since the birth of the boy so Henri left her alone. As long as she didn't bother him too much, he was fine with the situation. It was not a happy marriage but if you marry your secretary and then keep on treating her like one, what do you expect?

Henri settled the bankruptcy debts in order to take over David's company, and the Duponte name was restored within months. He gained sympathy from people, many of whom wanted to help him through this difficult time. He made sure that David's widow and the three children would be taken care of as well. Within a couple of years he was on top of his game, stronger and bigger than ever.

Unfortunately, David's wife became greedy and sued Henri for half of the company, stating that he took advantage of her husband's death, thus using the state of affairs for his own benefit. Though he knew that her accusations were groundless, he settled out of court, giving her a good chunk of money that would keep her happy for the rest of her life. He also made her sign a binding contract, making sure she would never ask for more in the future. That was the last time he saw her.

The test results came back after two days. Henri opened the envelope with shaky hands. He read the few lines quickly.

"Goddammit!" he shouted, "She is 99% my daughter."

Suddenly he felt a sharp pain in his chest that turned into uncomfortable pressure, moving towards his neck and left arm. Oh, no, he thought. This is a heart attack! He froze, unable to move or call for help. Suddenly, he broke out in cold sweat and tumbled to the floor.

Henri woke up in the hospital with no clue how he got there. Next to him was his son Maxence, holding his father's hand, looking worried.

"Papa," he said in French. "How are you feeling? Are you okay? Can you hear me? Say something."

Henri squeezed his son's hand for an answer, trying to force a smile to his face but unable to do so. His hand softened and turned weak.

"Can I get you anything?" Maxence continued. "Tell me what you need."

The drugs they gave Henry caused him to doze off immediately. Maxence stayed at his side day and night. In his pocket he had a letter that he found by his father's lifeless body on the floor. Who was the DNA test for? Only Henri's name was on the paper. Who was the other person? Maxence wanted answers and he wanted them fast.

His mother, Mathilda came to the hospital as soon as Maxence called but stayed only few hours as the doctors advised her that Henri would be asleep for several days.

Outside the door, a worried Mike paced back and forth in the corridors, his face pinched with worry. It was the first time in many years that he felt hopeless, not able to help his boss when in need. At that moment he realized the meaning of close friendships. Fearing that he might lose not only an employer but also a dear friend, saddened him. Though he didn't believe in God, that night he prayed for Henry and for himself.

Doctor Pierre Pichou, a childhood friend of Henri's and his doctor for more than three decades, entered the room carrying medical reports. Though the doctor had retired 10 years ago, he was still on call for Henri and his family. Besides that, he knew everyone and everyone knew him. At least half of the doctors in Geneva had been his students at some stage in their carrier.

"Good morning Henri. How are you feeling today?" he asked with a smile. "Better, I hope."

"What happened to me?" Henri asked.

"You had a heart attack my friend. But you will be fine, we took care of it." He didn't sound happy though, so Henri sensed that something was bothering him.

"Henri, we have known each other all our lives so I need to be honest with you, this is not easy to say," he paused for a moment.

"What is it Pierre?"

"Well, we made all the tests, including the scans,

just to be sure what was going on with you, and unfortunately we discovered that you have stage four pancreatic cancer. I am so sorry to tell you this, truly sorry."

"Stage four? Are you sure? How is that possible as I didn't have any symptoms? I lost some weight lately but that's all."

"Pancreatic cancer can be difficult to discover until it's too late," the doctor explained to Henri. "We rarely see it until it spreads to other organs in your body. Your cancer has metastasized to your liver and few other places."

"How bad is it?" he asked looking down at his hands. "How long do I have?"

"Hard to say, maybe one to three months," he said with a shaky voice. "In the lottery of cancers, you picked the most lethal one. We can't operate but we can do chemo and radiation. There is still hope Henri, we have experimental trials with bone marrow transplant that have proven effective in similar cases. But you will need a donor."

Henri was silent, trying to digest the news. Doctor Pichou hesitated for a moment and then said,

"Shall I talk to Maxence?"

"No," Henri responded. "Let me think about this. Say nothing to anyone."

"As you wish Henri."

As Henri lay in his hospital bed, he reflected on his life. No regrets, he thought. There is no point to regret anything. Would he have changed anything? Made different choices? Sure, he had made some mistakes. Like all people do. These events made him who he is today; a confident and a very wealthy person, highly respected in the community. What else could you wish for? He had everything a person could dream for. So why was he unhappy?

Looking back on his life, he realized the last time he was truly happy was with Cecilia, Anna's mother, that summer in Cannes. Why did he let her go? Why didn't he go to Sweden to get her back? He thought of her often but then David died and things changed. Life changed.

Doctor Pichou was back the next day, trying to convince Henri about the bone marrow transplant.

"Let me test Maxence, Henri. Let me see if he is a good candidate," he pleaded with him. "This could give you another 10 to 15 years, maybe even 20. Please, Henri." The doctor's eyes narrowed on Henri, the seriousness of the situation showing on his face.

"How dangerous is this procedure? And is it painful? I don't want Maxence to suffer."

"He will be fine Henri, no pain and no suffering. It's done under anesthesia. We put a needle into his pelvic bone and withdraw liquid marrow. There will be no risk for him and absolutely no pain. It will take him a few weeks to replenish the marrow and then he will be as good as new," he added with a smile. "He will have to stay in the hospital for few days after so we can watch him. He'll be on antibiotics to eliminate possible infections or complications as his immune system will be lowered.

"So what you take from him you put inside me? Where?"

"If he is a match, we take the marrow, clean it and inject it into your bloodstream by the central venous catheter. Your blood will know what to do with it, transporting the marrow, or stem cells as we also call them, to your bones. Once there, you will start producing healthy blood cells that will attack your pancreatic tumors, hopefully destroying them completely. That's the plan, anyhow," Pierre added.

"I will have to tell him myself then," Henri responded, feeling a little better by knowing that Maxence will be fine with the painless procedure.

Maxence was back with Henri the same afternoon. Henri explained the situation to him, stressing that he didn't have to do it if he felt uncomfortable or uncertain about it. Maxence was in shock. Not because of the transplant but because Henri had cancer and was dying. Of course, he would do it, he said without hesitation. We are family, this is what you do for your family. But he also wanted to know about the letter he had found next to his father's lifeless body. What was that about? Henri had no choice but to explain the DNA test and come clean about Anna. After all, she was Maxence's half-sister.

Henri told him about the summer in Cannes, about Cecilia and her pregnancy that he was unaware of for so many years. He told him that Mike went to Sweden to watch her and to find more information about her. And finally, Henri told his son not to say anything to his mother. Mathilda had enough on her plate right now as it was.

Maxence was stunned. First cancer and then this? WTF! I have a younger sister? She is five years younger than me. So I was four when my father had an affair with her mother. This is crazy. He didn't want to be judgmental towards his father but how could he not? His father was the smartest person he knew so how could he be so stupid to get another woman pregnant while married to his mother? This didn't make sense to Maxence. Something is not right here, he thought.

Did his father have a midlife crisis at the time? Why would he betray Mom? And what was going to happen now? Father is ill, God knows if he will live and for how long, so I will have to run the business. And who is this Anna? What does she want from us? There were many questions in Maxence's head.

Few days later doctor Pichou was back at Henri's side.

"Henri, I have something important to tell you," he said solemnly. "This is not good, I'm afraid."

"What is it Pierre?"

"Well, the test results came back and unfortunately Maxence is not a match for the transplant. I'm so sorry. But we can put you on the waiting list and see if any donors come up. Sadly, the wait can be long and we don't have so much time," he said. He looked seriously into Henri's face. "There is another thing you ought to know. I am telling you this because you are my friend Henri," he paused for a moment.

"What is it Pierre? Give it to me straight."

"Hmm," doctor Pichou hesitated, not sure how to proceed as Henri just suffered a heart attack and he didn't want to cause another one. "We did some additional testing on Maxence just to be certain he wasn't suitable as a donor, and the lab results that came back were remarkable, not as we expected."

"What do you mean? Is he sick?" Henri was impatient now.

"From the results, we concluded that Maxence is not your son Henri. I'm so sorry to tell you this."

Henri looked at his friend with astonishment.

"You are joking, right?" How was this even possible? Maxence was his only child, the son that he had raised from birth, the only heir after Henri to the Duponte fortune. "If he is not my son then whose son is he?"

"You will have to ask Mathilda, hopefully she knows," the doctor responded relieved that the difficult task of telling his friend was over. What a mess he thought. When it rains it pours. He used to be envious of Henri's extravagant lifestyle with private jets, yachts and over the top exclusive cars. Not anymore. He wouldn't trade his good health for any money in the world. Of course, the money could buy you the best medical care available, maybe even prolong your life but no, Pierre would rather fly commercial and drive his 6-year-old Range Rover. Besides that, the wealthy people he knew were always miserable. They constantly had some problems and were never happy with what they got. More money they earned, more expenses they had. What a life.

Mathilda sat beside Henri's bed complaining about the Geneva traffic. It took her 45 minutes to get to the hospital, a journey that usually takes only 15, and she wasn't happy about it. She always had something to complain about, never happy with her life. And now with Henri in the hospital, her life was pure hell, a condition that she continually needed to convey to her husband. Finally, after listening to her for half an hour, a frustrated Henri asked her about Maxence. As the tests were clear, there was no way she would deny him the truth, he thought.

Mathilda was taken aback. At first she didn't know what to say. In a way she was happy that the truth finally came out but on the other side, she was scared that her loving son and heir to the Duponte throne could be dethroned. The good thing was that she and Maxence were the only family that Henri had left so Maxence was the given successor to the Duponte Empire.

"Let me explain Henri," Mathilda said cautiously. "We tried for many years to get pregnant and nothing happened. Finally I became desperate; you know I was over 35 by then, so when you were away in New York, I had a one night stand with a random guy that looked like you. I never saw him again. And he doesn't know about Maxence. So for me, he is your son and no one else's."

"Do you know his name?" Henri asked. "Who was this guy?"

"No, I know nothing about him. He was from out of town, visiting for a conference. I think he was married because he had a wedding ring. We had a few drinks at a bar and then went back to his hotel room. It was all very quick you know. Luckily I got pregnant and when I told you, you were so happy that I didn't know how to tell you the truth. As far as I was concerned, Maxence was our son. The other guy was just a sperm donor. He meant nothing to me." She paused before adding, "You were not an angel yourself Henri, let's be honest about it. How many affairs did you have? I know at least four or five. Correct me if I'm wrong."

No, she was not wrong about that. Henri had had his share of extramarital affairs, many more than what she knew about. And he had no intention of telling her about Anna. A man in his position, with great wealth and power, was always surrounded by beautiful women who were keen to please him. Money was like honey to bees, a never ending string of wannabes, so Henri could have any woman he wanted. It was easy when your name was Duponte. His father was the same, as far as Henri could remember, his parents always fought about his dad's affairs. His mother was never happy, she seemed depressed. The doctor was often visiting, giving her some kind of pills. When she wasn't depressed, she had a migraine, which was even worse because then she stayed in her dark bedroom for days and no one could disturb her. That was not a happy childhood.

So, was Mathilda depressed because of Henri's affairs or was Henri unfaithful because of Mathilda's depression? Like the chicken and the egg story, which came first? Henri was shocked, as the thought of rightful fatherhood had never crossed his mind. He had raised him the best he could. If Mathilda was telling the truth, then Henri was the only father that Maxence knew of.

"Please don't tell him," Mathilda pleaded. "It would kill him, he loves you so much."

Maxence was back at the hospital the next morning.

"I've been thinking Dad, about this Anna in Sweden. Let's bring her here and test her. Maybe she is a match. That would solve the problem. What do you think?"

Henri's face fell.

"She will think we contacted her only for that.

Besides it's unethical. I can't do it."

"Yes, you can," Maxence insisted. "Don't you see this was perfect timing? Everything happens for a reason. She was sent to you by God. Why not take your chance? Please Dad."

"No," Henri said sternly. "You can call her to come here but only to meet me and nothing else. No testing for bone marrow."

"We will have to test her anyhow as she doesn't know about the DNA test you made. I'm sure she wants that, so at the same time Pierre can see if she is a match. Just to check and then you can make your decision," Maxence said, trying to persuade his dad.

Henri watched Maxence closely. The way the boy spoke, walked and gestured. The way he thought and argued his case. All these years Henri assumed that the boy was a Duponte, a born leader and conqueror, just like Henri. Were these traits in his DNA or were they modeled by Henri? Are babies born *tabula rasa*, a blank slate, or do they bring innate knowledge at birth? The nature versus nurture debate. Was John Locke right or wrong?

"Call her tonight and ask her to come," Henri finally said to Maxence. "Ask Clotilde to book her a ticket for tomorrow. But not a word about donating anything. I want to meet her before my time is out. And I want you to be nice to her."

"Yes Dad, I will. Where will she stay? We can't bring her home, Mom would have a fit," Maxence said, concern in his voice.

"Let me talk to Princess Sobieski," Henri responded. "Since her husband died she has been lonely. She might like to have company for a few days. I will call her tomorrow morning."

Princess Marie Sobieski was a true blue-blooded princess. Though she was born and bred in Geneva, her family originated from the Polish aristocracy, spanning back to the 15th and 16th centuries.

One of her ancestors was the Polish King Jan Sobieski, another one was the British King James, officially the king of England, Scotland and Ireland. Forced to foreign exile, the Sobieski family originally settled in France but later moved to the neighboring Geneva, in the French part of Switzerland. They belonged to the Bourgeoisie de Genève, the old Geneva families – the aristocrats. There were only a few of them left nowadays, so the princess was well regarded in the society, like a rare precious flower in the desert.

The fact that she was rich contributed of course but she was one of the last well-mannered, sophisticated and courteous ladies alive. She was always polite to everyone, from the help to kings and queens. Her mother taught her that politeness is the first virtue to be learned as it doesn't come naturally to us, it has to be practiced until you master it gracefully.

Now at 80 years of age, the princess mastered many more virtues as she was the epitome of elegance and good taste, the old school one that you rarely see today. She was always immaculately dressed in the most classic haute couture from Chanel or Dior.

Her beautiful face, slightly wrinkled yet untouched by plastic surgery, was well-maintained by monthly facials. Her minimal make-up routine was classy yet subtle. Her silver hair always in place, beautifully coiffed by her beloved hairdresser Fabrice. She was pure perfection. But she was lonely.

Despite her spectacular beauty and good fortune in life, the princess was in pain because more than 50 years ago she lost her only child at birth. Her little baby daughter Alexandra was born premature due to complications with the placenta. She lived only for a minute. The princess almost bled to death, so in order to save her life the doctors performed a hysterectomy, removal of her uterus, making her unable to carry another child.

She was traumatized for several years and though her husband wanted to adopt a baby, the princess refused. One day he came home with a puppy. The princess fell instantly in love with the little Chihuahua girl and the two became promptly inseparable. She treated the puppy as her baby girl.

Many years passed and few Chihuahuas followed, as they only live 12 to 15 years. The princess always made sure to get a new beige female puppy as soon as the old one died. On her bedroom walls she kept oil paintings of each of her darling Chihuahuas. They were her guardian angels.

The current Chihuahua named Coco, after Coco Chanel, her favorite brand of clothes, shoes and bags, followed the princess everywhere. She had her own

Chanel bag and of course Chanel clothes. Few people rolled their eyes and made signs behind the princess' back but it didn't become her. She loved her little beige Chihuahua dearly, with her apple head, flat nose, big eyes and ears, and her tiny little legs that weren't made for walking. She carried her in the tan colored Chanel bag wherever they went. When invitations to functions arrived by post they were addressed to Her Royal Highness Princess Sobieski & Coco Sobieski. Coco always had her own seat at the table or on the plane. She was treated like a royalty.

6

GOTHENBURG, SWEDEN

Anna's phone rang just after 11 p.m. When she saw a Swiss number, starting with +41, her heart skipped a bit. Is this him? she thought. Is my father finally calling me? She was so nervous she almost dropped the phone.

"Hello," she practically whispered.

"Hi, is this Anna?" Maxence asked.

"Yes, this is Anna."

"Hi Anna, my name is Maxence Duponte. I'm Henri Duponte's son. Sorry for calling you this late but my father is not well and he asked me to call you urgently.

"Okay…" she was not sure what to say next so she waited.

"So my father would like to meet you and because he is not well, he would like you to come tomorrow already. Is that possible for you? We will send you a ticket of course."

"Ohh, I don't know, this was a surprise, I didn't

expect this," she felt awkward speaking English.

"Well, think about it and let me know by tomorrow morning. Text me at the number on your phone. And sorry again for my intrusion. Have a good night Anna and I hope to see you tomorrow in Geneva."

"Wait a second!" Anna came to her senses. "How is he? Your father? What happened to him?"

"He had a heart attack a few days ago but we are hoping he will recover soon."

"Okay, I will let you know tomorrow," Anna responded. "Goodnight."

She immediately called Elin and told her about the phone call.

"What shall I do? Should I go tomorrow?"

"Of course you should, you have to meet him. Think, if he dies soon, you will regret delaying the trip."

So, the next morning Anna texted Maxence that she would come to Geneva. She had never been to Switzerland before so she didn't know much about the country. "I need to Google this," she said to herself. Where exactly is Switzerland and where is Geneva? Oh no, they speak French. She knew some German from school but only few words of French. They will think that I'm stupid because I don't speak French.

She learned that Geneva is the second largest city in Switzerland, after Zurich, just like Gothenburg is the second largest city after Stockholm. The population of canton Geneva is half a million, more or less same as Gothenburg. Geneva has a lake with a 140 meters high fountain, called *Jet d'Eau* which means water jet. Anna had seen this fountain before in some photos online. Often, there was a mountain in the background, the *Mont Blanc*, the tallest peak of the French Alps.

Gothenburg doesn't have a fountain but it has the sea and the water canals in the inner city. She also learned that in Geneva there are as many banks as there are pubs in London. How is that even possible? Do people eat money there? Why so many banks?

The currency is Swiss Franc with exchange rate of one franc to eight Swedish Kronas. The most valuable note in Europe is the Swiss 1,000 francs note. Wow, that's lot of money, she thought.

7

GENEVA, SWITZERLAND

Maxence texted her that a driver would meet her at the Geneva airport. After collecting her luggage, she passed the customs and saw a middle aged man holding a sign with Ms. Andersson written on it. That's me, she thought.

"Hello," she said shyly to the man. "I'm Anna Andersson."

"Great," he responded in English. "Welcome to Geneva. I'm Mr. Duponte's driver. Let me take your bag mademoiselle." He led her to the exit door through the crowded arrival hall. "Sorry mademoiselle but this place is always busy. It's a nightmare to find a parking place close by. Please follow me."

As they made their way toward the exit, she heard a male voice calling her name.

"Anna? Is that you?"

She turned around to see a very handsome young man. He was tall with the most beautiful blue eyes she had ever seen in a man. She looked into his eyes and froze, like the time stood still and nothing else around them mattered. She couldn't utter a word to this gorgeous man. He was wearing blue jeans and a light blue Ralph Lauren polo shirt, which only accented the blueness of his eyes.

"Hi, I'm Maxence, your half brother," he said while moving forward to kiss her on her cheek. He did it three times, the way they do it in Switzerland. This felt strange to Anna as in Sweden people don't kiss each other, especially when they first met.

"Hello, nice to meet you," she finally said shaking with excitement. He seemed to have a profound impact on her, something that she never experienced before in her life. This is your brother silly you, she thought. Behave properly! How can you be so attracted to your own brother? This is wrong.

"Sorry I'm late but the traffic…" she didn't hear the rest of his sentence because a large group of Chinese tourists crossed their path.

"Please come with me. Let my driver take your luggage because my car doesn't have the space for it."

Oh, what are you driving then? A tricycle? Even my small Mini can fit a suitcase, she thought.

"We need to go to the second floor, to the departure hall. There are fewer people there at this time so I parked my car just outside the door."

As they took the escalator she stood close to him, still shivering with excitement. Cool off, please, put yourself together silly girl. She liked his smell, hell she liked everything about him.

"How was your flight?" he asked.

"Good," she said. That's it? Good? I should say something more but I can't. Actually, I have been travelling all day because I had to go to Copenhagen first in order to get here. So I'm not as fresh as you are, and I'm tired, she thought.

As they got to the street outside the terminal, they saw a large group of people surrounding a sports car. Everyone was taking selfies with the dark blue vehicle. A dismayed looking Maxence made his way to the passenger door, opening it for her.

"Please sit down," he said while holding the door.

So this is the car without the boot, she thought, how practical. How far can you go without a luggage? Or is your driver always following you in another car?

The inside of the car looked like a space ship. The leather seats had quilted stitching, similar to a Chanel bag. The integrated headrest had the name *Chiron* embroidered in blue letters. There was another *Chiron* on the side leather panel. Anna had never seen a car like this before.

"Nice car," she said smiling.

"Thank you," Maxence replied proudly. "It's brand new. I just collected it from the garage, that's why I was late."

"It must be a very special car as so many people were taking pictures of it," Anna said. The crowd was still taking photos as the car left the airport.

"Yes, indeed. There are only 500 Bugatti Chirons made and each car cost 2.5 million euro."

"Wow, that's a lot of money for a car. Is it worth it?"

"You bet it's worth it. I love it. There are only two cars like this in Geneva. It can go from zero to 400 kilometers in 32 seconds. It has an eight liter w16 engine with 1,500 horsepower."

Anna noticed the speedometer showing 500 kilometer per hour as the maximum speed.

"So how fast can you drive in Switzerland?" She knew that maximum speed in Sweden was 120 on the motorway.

"The fastest you can drive in Switzerland is 120 but only on the motorway," he said. "Next weekend I'm going to drive on a track in Dijon in France. Maybe you can come with me?"

"Sure, that would be fun. And how is your dad doing?" She didn't want to say *our* dad until she had met him in person.

"Still the same I'm afraid," he said solemnly. "We are going to see him now. He is excited to meet you. He told me that your mom passed away a few months ago. Sorry to hear that. It must have been difficult for you to deal with."

"Yes, it was," she said, her voice barely audible. She was nervous to meet her father for the first time. After all these years she was finally going to get to know him. And all the time she believed that he was dead. Growing without a dad was hard. She always felt like a part of her was missing. The fact that her mother was unwilling to share any information about him made it even worse. Even though Elin's dad was an alcoholic, at least she had a dad. Maybe that was the reason she became a tough and self-assured woman compared to Anna who was insecure most of the time. Meanwhile Elin was a fighter, Anna withdrew herself from conflicts as much as possible.

As they approached the hospital, Anna's anxiety grew. Her heart pounded so fast she was afraid Maxence might hear it. Please God help me, she prayed.

When they walked into Henri's hospital room, he recognized Anna from the photos Mike had sent. He thought she was more beautiful in person, with her dark hair and brown eyes. She resembled not only Henri, but also his late mother. So here she is, my daughter that I didn't know existed until couple of weeks ago. The thought was overwhelming to Henri.

Anna approached the bed slowly, trying not to get too emotional in front of Maxence. She could feel his eyes on her back. She tried to hold back her tears but suddenly when she looked into Henry's eyes, everything seemed so surreal; she burst into tears, her eyes blurred as the tears poured down her cheeks. She couldn't stop crying. Henry stretched his arms toward her.

"Come here," he said. "Let me give you a hug."

They embraced for a moment but then Anna withdrew from his arms feeling his weakness. His emaciated face didn't look well to her.

"Are you okay?" she said.

"I have been better. I'm very happy to finally meet you."

"Me too," said Anna. "Very happy."

Maxence was just behind her. "Let him rest now and we can come back tomorrow," he said to Anna. "Also, tomorrow morning we can make the necessary DNA tests to be sure that he is really your father. I'm sure you understand it's important." Maxence didn't care about the DNA, what he really wanted was the other test for bone marrow.

"Yes, of course. We need to be sure," Anna said. In her heart she knew the answer already. Henri Duponte was her long lost father. She knew that she could see herself in his eyes. She had finally found the missing piece of her.

"I have asked a dear friend of mine to take care of you while you are here, and while I'm in the hospital. Her name is princess Sobieski, she will take good care of you."

"Thank you but I would rather stay in a hotel if possible." She didn't feel comfortable staying with strangers.

"Out of the question," Henri responded. "You are family and we are responsible for you. You will have your own room and all the comforts of a five star hotel with the princess. Maxence, please escort Anna. I will see you tomorrow."

Maxence pulled his car in front of an old building in the centre of the city, close to the Saint Pierre Cathedral.

"Your luggage is already here," he said, turning to Anna. "The princess is expecting us."

Anna couldn't wait to call Elin and tell her everything. She had already received a few messages from her friend asking how the meeting went.

Rosita, the Spanish maid, opened the door. Behind her a small Chihuahua wearing a pink dress started to bark frantically.

"Be quiet Coco," Maxence said to the dog. "Where is the princess?" he asked Rosita.

"She is in the living room waiting for you."

They made their way to a salon with large windows overlooking the city. Princess Sobieski greeted them with a smile.

"Maxence, so nice to see you," she kissed him on

his cheeks three times. "And you must be Anna. So happy to meet you my dear. Henri told me about you," she continued while kissing Anna as well.

"Will you stay for dinner Maxence?" she asked.

"Sorry, can't make it tonight, maybe another time. Have to dash now before the police tow my car."

"Oh yes, it wouldn't be the first time, would it?" she joked, knowing Maxence was notorious for parking in the wrong places.

"Then it's only you and me for dinner," she said to Anna. "Why don't you go freshen up and change so we can eat shortly? Rosita will show you to your room."

The princess dressed in a black evening dress with three rows of white pearls around her neck, had an elegance about her that proved she was truly a princess. The room smelled of Chanel N°5, her aunt Birgitta's favorite perfume. Anna was surprised that the princess also wore her shoes inside the apartment since everyone takes their shoes off at the entrance in Sweden, whether you were a visitor or the host. It's perceived as rude to keep the shoes on.

The princess lived on the top of the building in a spacious apartment that spanned through two floors. There was also a roof top with a large terrace from which one could see the lake with its spectacular fountain, lit in a blue color tonight. Anna's room had its own big bathroom with an adjoined walk-in closet. Subtle colors elegantly decorated the room and a four poster double bed was piled high with colorful pillows and cushions. On the opposite side of the room was a large sofa and table.

Yes, this is definitely nicer than a hotel room, she thought.

Anna texted Elin that she would call her after the dinner and quickly jumped into the shower. Then she unpacked a few things from her suitcase looking for something suitable to wear for the occasion. She didn't have a proper dress so she wore jeans with a white blouse and no shoes on. Let's do this the Swedish way, she thought.

Finding her way back to the salon wasn't easy as Anna didn't remember the layout of this vast apartment. She wandered through opulent rooms, one more lavish than the other. Large oil paintings framed in gilded ornament frames, portraying important people wearing crowns and tiaras, adorned the walls. Were they relatives of the princess? Anna had never seen such luxury before except on television. What was the name of the place outside of Paris? Palace of Versailles? Yes, she remembered the Swedish documentary, recognizing the gilded ornaments, the magnificent furniture and the beautiful tapestry. For a moment she thought she was transferred to a Hollywood movie set.

"Wow, this is awesome!"

Suddenly she saw Coco in front of her.

"Hello little one, where is the princess? Can you show me the way?"

Coco looked at her with big eyes, her tail wagging happily as if she understood Anna. The dog turned and ran toward the dining room where the princess was waiting for her.

"I'm so happy to have you as my guest," she said when Anna entered the room.

"Thank you for having me," Anna said.

"Henri asked me to take good care of you Anna. It will be my pleasure. Henri is a good friend of mine. My late husband and Henri were very close."

Henri had told the princess that Anna needed some grooming before she was ready to be introduced to the Geneva society. She had good manners, he had said, but she lacked the *savoir vivre*. He had also asked her to take her shopping for some appropriate clothes, shoes and accessories. The girl had potential, he said but it would take some time to teach her proper etiquette. The princess was more than happy to take on this task as she liked Anna the moment she saw her tonight.

Rosita served the dinner. At first Anna thought that the maid would join them as there were three placemats on the table, but soon enough the princess put Coco in a special baby highchair so the tiny dog could see over the table. The dog had her own plate with a home cooked meal in front of her. This was the first time in Anna's life she had shared a table with a dog, dressed in a black evening dress, wearing a diamante encrusted dog collar, which was so beautiful it could be worn as a necklace, or given the size of Coco's neck, a bracelet.

The princess began peppering Anna with questions about Sweden. Apparently she had visited Stockholm on several occasions, mostly in conjunction with the Nobel ceremony dinners that take place in December. It was cold and very dark she said.

"Yes, the summers are much better in Sweden," Anna responded. "Winters are long and boring. This is the reason so many people in Scandinavia get depressed during the winter months."

"Yes, the SAD, the seasonal affective disorder," the princess said. "I read about this a few months ago. It's in Sweden that you have rooms in hospitals with special daylight lamps where people can sit and read for a few hours a day in the winter. Apparently this helps a lot if you have depressive tendencies. And is it true what they write about the refugees in Sweden?"

"What do they write here?" Anna wanted to know.

"That there are so many of them over there that they cause huge problems. That 70% of the resent refugees are young men. Some of them pretend to be much younger than they are in order to get permission to stay because young adults below the age of 18 get it automatically." She paused to take a bite of food while the maid collected a few dishes.

"Then there is plenty of violence and rapes of the Swedish girls. Have you seen any of that? It sounds scary to me."

Yes, it was scary to Anna as well but in Sweden you are not suppose to talk about these things or you are considered a racist. The official version, beside the humanitarian need to help the less fortunate people, is that immigration is good for the country and its economy. The fact that it costs billions of kronas every year is explained by the left-wing politicians as money going back to the Swedish society, because the refugees spend it in the country.

Their lodging and living expenses benefit the Swedish people, especially the few known characters who made a fortune on renting out their hotel rooms to them. But the Swedish people are scared when they see so many jobless immigrants on the streets. The women are frightened even more due to several rape reports connected to the immigrants. The police came out with statements urging the female population to cover up so these people coming from other cultures would feel less tempted to commit sexual crime. Soon they will ask us to wear burqas Anna thought. This is insane.

"Yes, it's scary but we are not suppose to talk about it. They cover it up. The government."

"Okay then, tell me about yourself. I'm curious about you."

"I grew up in Gothenburg on the west coast of Sweden. I never knew my father as my mom didn't want to talk about him. She told me that he died long time ago."

"Do you know why she said that?"

"No idea" Anna said. "So when my mom died earlier this year, her sister told me about my dad and I wrote him a letter."

"I'm very glad you did so we could meet." The princess smiled. "Have some sleep now as Henri told me you will have the blood test tomorrow morning at the hospital. Maxence will pick you up at eight in the morning. Remember, you can't eat anything before the test, only drink water."

Anna said good night to the princess and went back to her room. Finally she could call Elin to tell her what happened. That her dad looked really sick but that he was happy to meet her. She omitted the fact about her attraction to Maxence though, as she felt ashamed about her feelings. She felt like an incestuous pervert. *He is your brother for God's sake, get a grip girl,* she reprimand herself.

Next morning Maxence showed up 10 minutes before eight o'clock to pick her up. He was in a good mood. He hoped that Anna was a perfect match for donating bone marrow for his father. *I need to be nice to her,* he thought. *She is the last chance that we have to make him better.*

Anna got into his car, which today was a red Ferrari Laferrari, another sports car that presumably cost a fortune.

"How much is this one?" she asked after settling into the seat.

"Two million Swiss francs and it has 950 horsepower," he answered smugly. "There were only 500 cars made of this model."

His confidence was daunting to her. *This guy is so self-assured that he thinks he owns the world. It's only a car, dude. Relax.* Besides, the car felt uncomfortable to her. It was so low that she was sitting almost on the ground. *Not a good feeling at all, you must be a man to like this,* she thought. The red leather seats were equipped with four-point harness looking seat belts, something you would strap in a toddler into a buggy. Though they had two shoulder pads with the yellow Ferrari logo on, they were still uncomfortable on top of her boobs. *Must be a man who designed this,* she thought. *Or maybe this car was made for flat-chested women only?*

Thankfully, it was a short ride to the hospital.

Since her mother's passing, Anna dreaded hospitals. They reminded her of death. She was also afraid of needles but there was no way to get away from it now as she needed to know for sure that Maxence's dad was her father as well.

The nurse collected a few vials of blood from Anna's arm. Why so much blood for a DNA test, Anna thought. The way she remembered it, the test was done by swabbing the inside of the mouth, or at least that's how she saw it on TV.

She asked Maxence who explained it to her. "The blood test is more accurate and much faster. They take a few vials to be sure," he lied as he knew precisely that the additional tubes were for something else. Something that she was unaware of.

"So how long does it take to get the results?" Anna asked.

"Two to three days," the nurse answered. "Now you should go to the cafeteria and have some breakfast."

The hospital's cafeteria looked much different than the Swedish hospital where her mother was treated and there Anna spent several months visiting. In the Swiss hospital they sold wine bottles next to the sandwiches. Really? This was unusual to her as in Sweden you couldn't buy wine in regular shops or cafeterias, only in specially designed shops called Systembolaget. These shops have the monopoly on alcoholic spirits over 3.5% and are owned by the government. You have to be over 20 years old to buy there, though restaurants will serve alcohol to 18 year olds and above. So in Switzerland drinking wine is like drinking juice in Sweden, she thought. Strange, because until now she hadn't seen any drunk people in the street.

Anna ate her breakfast alone as Maxence had already eaten at home and went up to see his father. She joined them when she was done and saw that Henri was looking better today.

"You survived the blood test?" Henri made an attempt at a joke. Maxence must have told him how scared she was.

"Ehh, I don't like needles," she said feeling ashamed that she was such a sissy about it. "I don't feel comfortable in hospitals."

"Who does?" Henri responded with a smile. "So come sit here with me. Tell me about yourself."

Anna didn't know where to start. Should she tell him about all these years she felt lonely without a father? Or the feeling of abandonment that followed her trough her life? The anger, thinking her father didn't care about her or didn't even try to find her? The sorrow when she saw other children's dads playing with them? The tears she cried when her mother told her that he had died? Should she tell him about the anguish it caused her? No, she wanted to stay positive, she wanted him to like her. Besides that, the man was sick so there was no reason to make his condition worse.

After an hour they were told by the nurse to leave as Henri needed to rest so Maxence drove Anna to the apartment.

65

The princess was delighted to see Anna again. Since her husband passed away five years ago she felt lonely in her large apartment. She had Rosita of course but the maid was acting older than her age; going to bed early and running to church every Sunday. And how much can you talk to Coco? She loved the dog dearly but there was not much conversation going on between them.

"Today is such a lovely day," she said to Anna. "Let's go shopping. Your dad is paying so make the most of it."

"Really? That's wonderful!" Anna grinned like a kid going to a candy store. "Can I buy anything I want?"

"I think so. He didn't mention any limit," the princess said, a smile spread across her face. "But before we do that, let's have a haircut and a mani/pedi."

"Mani/pedi?" Anna asked not sure what that meant.

"Manicure and pedicure. Your nails," the princess explained. "Every woman needs that to feel better."

"Okay, let's go," Anna said, ready to go.

They arrived at the Kempinski hotel where the door-man greeted them with a big smile.

"Good afternoon Princess Sobieski, so nice to see you again."

"Oh, hello Bertrand" she said, looking genuinely happy to see him. "How is your wife these days? I hope better."

"Yes, she is. Thank you for asking."

He ran ahead to open the side door for them.

"I don't like the revolving doors," the princess said

to Anna, "So let's take this one here."

Note to self – avoid revolving doors. Why? Did anything happen in the past? Will ask later.

From the doorman to the reception clerks, everyone seemed to know the princess. They took the lift to the second floor where salon Damien was located.

Fabrice, a tall handsome man in his early 40s, with short blonde hair and lovely hazel eyes, greeted them at the door. He was dressed in smart black jeans, Gucci belt and a white slim-cut shirt.

"Bonjour princesse, comment allez vous? And who is this beautiful lady?" he asked in French turning toward Anna.

"May I introduce you to my niece Anna?" the princess said to Fabrice. "Anna, this is Fabrice. He has been my hairdresser forever," she said smiling.

"Enchanté," Fabrice replied politely. "What can I do for you today?"

"Anna needs a makeover. What do you suggest?"

He took the elastic out of her pony tail and let her hair fall down as he ran his fingers through it. He looked carefully at her face from every angle.

"Let's do a haircut, keeping the length but layering it from here to make more volume," he said putting his hand at her neck to show where the layers would start. "And we need to put some highlights here." He pointed toward the top of her head. "Not too much, just a subtle hint of caramel. It will look great. Let me show you some photos so you know what I'm talking about." He took out his phone to show Anna a few pictures. "What do you think?" he asked.

"Yes." Anna liked what she saw. "Let's do it."

Her enthusiasm showed on her smiling face. This was her first visit at a high-end hair salon, well, any salon to be correct. She felt good, liking the attention she was getting.

Princess Sobieski ordered a fruit platter and two glasses of Dom Pérignon champagne. "Let's enjoy this," she said to Anna with a smile. "Cheers!"

Within minutes two women arrived pushing small trolleys on wheels containing an assortment of nail polishes. "Please make your choice, miss Sobieski," they said to Anna. "One for manicure and one for pedicure, or would you like same color for both?"

"Oh, my name is not Sobieski, just call me Anna," she replied embarrassed glancing at the princess who was seated with Coco next to the window, chatting happily to another lady and not aware of the conversation.

"Let me see," Anna glanced at the trolley with OPI nail polishes. What did the princess say about nail colors on the way here? She tried to remember. Red on toes and French tips on hands? Or was it beige on hands? Definitely red on toes, yes. She looked at the princess again, hoping for assistance as there were at least 10 different red shades on the trolley. This is so hard, she thought. How does Elin do it? But then again, Elin did not have the conservative look with her bold glittering colors or the Swarovski crystals on her stiletto shaped nails, the latest craze of the year. Anna's nails were natural oval shaped and rather short compared to Elin's. She rarely painted her nails, she preferred them natural and clean, just like her late mom's.

Princess Sobieski noticed Anna's puzzled face and came forward to help her.

"Let's choose together," she said. "What colors do you like?"

Anna looked at the princess' hands. Her nails were subtle beige, barely noticeable.

"Just like yours," she said looking at her nails. "What color do you use?"

"I think it's this one here," the princess pointed at a bottle with beige color. "Try this one."

"Okay, I like it." Anna took the bottle, relieved to have found the perfect color. Now she had to choose another one for her feet.

"Red for the toes?" she asked the princess.

"Yes, why not?" The princess looked over the red shades. "I like this one here and also this one here is nice," she said, picking up two shades. "What do you think?"

Anna liked them both. They were both bright red, the first one a fire engine red and the second one a blood red, a tough choice to make. She went for the blood red which was more muted.

"Good choice," the princess said and went back to her seat by the window.

Fabrice was back with another trolley, this one containing the hair color in a bowl, a color brush and a pile of aluminum foil squares.

"Are you ready?" he said smiling.

Anna took another sip from her glass of champagne. "Yes, I am." She said putting her glass down on the mirrored table in front of her.

"Good. Let me turn the chair around so the two ladies here can work on your feet and hands, meanwhile I will do your hair. Are you comfortable like this?"

"Yes, sure." Anna wasn't sure how this set up was going to work out. She had never been attended to by three people at the same time. Her feet were inside a plastic square basin with warm water and her hands inside a bowl with soapy water. Meanwhile Fabrice stood behind her, putting paint on thin strips of her hair, covering them with aluminum foil. The pedicure lady sat in front of Anna and the manicure lady on her side.

Oh, I wish someone could take a picture with my phone so I could send it to Elin, she thought, but was too embarrassed to even suggest such a thing to anyone.

It took Fabrice two hours for the color, wash, hair cut and blow dry. The end result was stunning.

"Bellissima!" Fabrice declared with pride. "You are the most beautiful woman in Geneva. After you princess, of course," he added looking at them both.

"Now we need the maquillage, or makeup as you say in English."

The makeup artist arrived promptly with her kit. She put primer and foundation on Anna's face, working it in with a beauty blender; a small egg-shaped pink sponge. Then she plucked the eyebrows, trimmed them a little and filled them in with a brown pencil. She made Anna's eyes look even bigger than before with several muted eyeshadows and plenty of black mascara. Lastly, she lined her lips and finished with a bold dark red color called Ruby Woo by Mac, a classic retro matte finish lipstick.

"What do you think? Do you like it?" the makeup artist asked Anna when she was done.

"Yes, I like it very much but the lips are too dark for me." Anna didn't feel comfortable with her bold red lips. Oh God, she thought, everyone will be looking at me. She wanted to run to the bathroom and wipe the lipstick off as soon as possible.

"No problem," Fabrice said. "We can change the color to a nude one if you prefer."

"Yes, please," Anna said politely, massively relieved to get rid of the red color. What she needed now was to take a couple of selfies for Elin. The power of makeup, she thought looking in the mirror, barely recognizing herself. It will take me some time to get used to it.

The princess was happy with Anna's transformation. "Well done Fabrice," she said praising his work. "You have outdone yourself again." Then she asked for a detailed list of all products that the makeup artist had used on Anna.

"We need to buy these for Anna. Let's go shopping."

They went to Globus, the department store on Rue du Rhône, the main shopping street in Geneva. Anna noticed the fashionable signs of Chanel, Hermès, Versace, Armani, Gucci, Dior, Louis Vuitton, Cartier, Rolex and a plethora of jewelers on the prestigious street. They were all concentrated here. Makes shopping easy, she thought.

The makeup sales assistant in Globus took their list and told them to come back in a couple of hours to collect the items. If they didn't have something on the list she would substitute with a similar one.

"Perfect," said the princess. "Now we can go buy shoes."

Anna couldn't help but take a glance at herself in every passing mirror. Wow, who's that girl? Is that me? She had a feeling that people were staring at her. Secretly she wished they would run into Maxence so he could see her now, because tomorrow she would be back to the old boring Anna again. She had no clue how to apply the makeup and in what order.

The princess noticed that men were looking at Anna with interest. She was young and beautiful, so of course they would notice her. One thing about aging, the princess knew, is that at a certain age you become *invisible*, you blend into the woodwork. Was it around 50 or was it even before? The men would gaze over her head like she didn't exist. Walking with Anna reminded her of her youth. She could feel the positive energy the girl exuded.

Standing in front of the Christian Louboutin shoe shop on Rue du Rhône, Anna's heart skipped a beat when she pulled out her phone to snap a picture for Elin. This is crazy, she thought, I'm looking at the holy grail of shoes, all red soles in their glory. If Elin could be here with me she would scream out of joy. She took a picture of the red crotch-high platform boots with steep stiletto heels. They looked like something a hooker would wear, like the ones Julia Roberts wore in *Pretty Woman* but not as shiny. And much higher for that matter. Who buys this stuff?

And for this price? Whose legs are this long? And so skinny?

She sent the photo to Elin with capture "Something for you?" Elin responded immediately "OMG!!!!!!!!!!!! Love these!!!!!!!!" Followed by several emojis.

"My friend loves the Louboutins," Anna said to princess Sobieski. "She has several pairs of this brand."

"That's nice," princess answered. "Can she walk in them?"

"Not too far," Anna said with a quirky smile. "They are rather uncomfortable."

"Yes, I know," the princess said. "I do own a few pairs of his classic pumps. I believe they are called the simple pump and Fifi. They have rounded toes though the best selling model is called Pigalle, with the pointed toe. Let's go inside and have a look."

Anna's face flushed and her heart sped the moment she stepped inside the store. Her eyes were wide as they scanned the room. This was her first visit ever to the Louboutin heaven. Some of the shoes were just insane; with spikes, crystals and platforms higher than 10 centimeters. A female shop assistant greeted them with a smile but let them look around in peace.

"Let me know if you need any help" she said politely. "And would you like a bowl of water for your dog?"

This is so not Sweden, Anna thought. Everyone here offers water to Coco, this would never happen in my country.

"You know Anna, this is quite funny; all the hype about his red soles," said the princess while they looked around in the store. "He said once in an interview that he got inspired by his assistant painting her nails in front of him with red nail polish. He grabbed the polish and painted the soles of the shoes, inventing the red sole look. This was in 1992, one year after he opened his own store in Paris. The funny part about this is that in the early 80s, so several years before the nail polish story, another shoe brand called Charles Jourdan was known for shoes with red soles. I had several pairs of CJ shoes at that time. Not only had they red soles but also red insoles. Remind me at home to show you a pair that I kept all these years. According to people that know Louboutin, he was working at Charles Jourdan in the 80s. So the question is; was it his idea or did he copy the red soles from Charles Jourdan?"

"Interesting," said Anna. "I didn't know about this. I will have to tell Elin."

"Every shoe here has red soles but Charles Jourdan's shoes were mixed; some had red soles and some had other colors. The only difference between CJ red soles and Louboutin's is a thin gold line on the CJ sole. I remember this clearly as I thought they looked extravagant at the time."

Speaking of extravagant, Anna had never seen so many opulent shoes before. Looking at the prices, her head started to spin. These are crazy expensive, she thought. A thousand francs for regular leather shoes and few thousands for the exotic skins like crocodile or lizard. This might be the reason that people regard them as a status symbol. Despite the high prices there was no lack of buying customers in the store. A young couple that spoke Russian had a pile of boxes on the floor. At the cashier there was a male customer paying for his shoes. Business was booming here.

"In 2008 Christian Louboutin applied for a patent in the U.S., a registered trademark for red soles," the princess continued with her story. "They gave it to him but when he tried to sue other shoe manufactures, Yves Saint Laurent among others, the U.S. judge ruled against him. Same happened here in Europe when he sued Zara in France and another shoe brand here in Switzerland. So anyone can produce red soles if they want to."

"Interesting," said Anna. "Why don't they then? Are they afraid of being sued?"

"Maybe they are, who knows? Let's have a look at the classic pumps here," the princess said pointing at the lower shelf in the corner, as if someone wanted to hide the *boring* models there. "You will need one pair of black and another one of beige. What is your size?"

"39." Anna responded with excitement in her voice.

"Then 39 and a half or even 40 will work for you because they are made for narrow feet so you have to go up a size, especially for the pointed toe ones like the Pigalle. They have a narrow toe box and the fit is tight so they might be painful if the size is too small."

"So you think my feet are wide?" Anna asked, looking down at her bulky feet. Compared to the princess with her tiny feet, Anna's feet looked enormous.

"Not at all," the princess said. "People in Sweden and Germany have wider feet than south Europeans. This is normal. Louboutin makes narrow shoes so the foot looks slimmer. Not everyone can wear his shoes. You need to try them on and see which model fits you best."

The sales assistant came back with several beige boxes. Déjà vu came to Anna's mind; Elin's closet. But this time it was Anna's turn. All these boxes just for her.

After trying on several pairs they decided on black pumps called "Pigalle." This is the iconic Louboutin style with pointed toe and 85 millimeter stiletto heel. A must for every fashionista. The second pair was beige "Simple Pump." These had a round toe and also 85 millimeter stiletto heel, the highest possible that Anna could wear without tipping over.

"These two are the basic ones that you need for now," the princess said. "They might not be very comfortable but for a couple of hours at a time they are fine. You must be careful where you step in these because the heels are tiny so you might scuff them especially when walking on uneven pavements or cobblestones. We have plenty of these in Geneva and I have ruined many expensive shoes because of that."

"Yes, for sure," Anna responded. "I will be careful." She was already worried as the thought of scraping them made her sick to her stomach.

"Let's go across the street to Jimmy Choo and see what they have there," the princess said, her face beaming. "Do you know the brand?"

"Not really," Anna said. She had seen the name in some fashion magazines but never seen the shoes in real life. Not even in Elin's closet.

"These were very popular some 20 years ago along with Manolo Blahniks. I used to go to London and buy 10 to 12 pairs of Manolos at a time as we didn't have them here in Geneva. I would also order them in the New York store and they would produce them in Italy and ship directly to me here in Geneva. Those were the days," she said smiling. "It's still hard to find them here. The closest store is in Paris."

"What is so special about Manolos?" Anna wanted to know.

"Manolos were the first iconic shoes due to the TV series *Sex and the City*. Carrie Bradshaw used to rave about them. They were her priciest possessions. His most popular shoe is the BB pump, named after the French actress Brigitte Bardot, a classic court shoe that comes in several heel heights. His shoes are sexy and sophisticated yet much more comfortable to wear than Louboutins or Choos. They are made for real women. The leather he uses is also softer, at least it feels like it compared to the sturdy Louboutins. He is also known for the kitten heel, a slightly curved shorter heel that you can find on his mules. So pretty," the princess sighed with pleasure.

"Oh, now I definitely need a pair of Manolos in my life," Anna said smiling.

"Yes, you do," the princess confirmed. "You know, I went to school with Manolo. He used to study here in Geneva. Such a nice man."

"Really?" Anna said in disbelief. The princess seemed to know everyone important, or at least know *of* them.

"He has always been consistent with his designs, making feminine shoes, never sneakers or wedges. He believes that sport shoes make our feet look ugly."

"But can you run in high heels? Is that what he wants?"

"No, of course not, but a real lady doesn't need to run, she trots along," the princess answered tongue in cheek.

Ha, this was funny since Anna couldn't imagine a life without her comfortable Converse sneakers.

"What shoe brand do you consider to be the best?" Anna asked.

"I usually buy Chanel, Stuart Weitzman or Ferragamo, it depends what I need them for. Gianvito Rossi and Valentino Rock Studs are very popular these days. But the most comfortable shoes that I own are made by the Italian brand Bruno Magli. Unfortunately, the company was sold some 15 years ago and their shoes have never been the same since. We used to have a big Bruno Magli shop on Rue du Rhône here in Geneva but they closed. Their leather was butter soft, it was like wearing slippers, yet they were elegant. Do you know that your Swedish Queen Silvia only wore Magli shoes before? Her shoe size is the same as mine, 37. We met a few times at dinner functions here in Geneva and once we wore exactly the same gold-colored Magli pumps. She told me that she had several pairs of the same model and so did I. We laughed about it. Funny how you get used to the good stuff in life. Comfortable shoes are important because they affect your wellbeing the most. If your feet hurt nothing feels good anymore. So always invest in good quality leather shoes. And bags of course."

"What is the most important thing to know about hand bags?" Anna asked. She knew that Elin's holy grail bag was the Hermès Birkin. She had been on the waiting list in the Paris store since last year, but still waiting for the call. When Stefan heard that the bag cost 8,000 euro he flipped out on her. She countered by telling him that what she really wanted was the crocodile Birkin with diamonds on the hardware but that bag cost 150,000 euro. So she *settled* for the basic model to save him some money. She knew how to play him.

"When it comes to bags," the princess said, "quality is the most important part. Always buy high-quality leather bags from known brands like Hermès and Chanel. I would say that Hermès is number one in leather goods. Nothing really compares to a Kelly or Birkin bag. These are the top bags to own. Then comes the classic Chanel flap bag. This bag has been made for decades but is still fashionable. They are expensive, of course, compared to other brands but they last forever. If you scratch a Hermès bag you can always bring it back to the store and they will fix it. Especially the shiny box leather that only looks better with age as it gets the famous patina look. A true classic."

"What's so special with the Birkin bag?" Anna asked the princess thinking about Elin's long wait. She would walk over broken glass to get it.

"Well, the bag was named after the actress Jane Birkin who travelled on the same plane as the chief executive of Hermès, Jean-Louis Dumas. This was in 1981. Jane told him that she needed a new bag that would hold everything yet look elegant. So he adapted the original Haut à Courroies (HAC) saddle bag that had been produced at Hermès since 1892. He made it a little shorter in the body because the bag was made to carry riding boots. He also made the handles a little longer and voila, the Birkin bag was born. So the Birkin is the HAC's little sister and a status symbol for wealthy people worldwide. Here in Europe the Hermès Kelly bag has always been regarded as the epitome of elegance and class. Named after princess Grace Kelly, the American actress who married prince Rainier of Monaco in 1956. Originally the bag was called *sac à dépêches* which means a messenger's bag but after princess Kelly was photographed carrying the bag in front of her stomach, to cover the pregnancy from the prying paparazzi, it was renamed the Kelly bag."

"Are there any Sobieski bags at Hermès?" Anna asked.

"Oh no, ha ha, what a thought," the princess answered amused. "I met Princess Kelly on few occasions and I must say that she rarely looked happy. There was a rumor that she drowned her sorrows in alcohol, though I never saw her drunk. Who knows what the real story was behind the closed doors. She was very beautiful though."

What a story, Anna thought. The princess had had such an exciting life. What a remarkable woman she is.

"So what is the difference between the Birkin and a Kelly bag? And why are they so expensive? What makes them so different from other bags?" Anna asked.

"The Birkin bag is bulkier, like a shopping tote. It has two handles and the Kelly bag has only one. So you carry the Birkin on your arm. The Kelly bag comes with a detachable shoulder strap making it easy to carry on your shoulder so you have both hands free. I find it more practical but also more elegant than the Birkin. They cost the same by the way. In the last decade, the Birkin became highly popular among the New York Upper East Side ladies, making it a sign of wealth. The price tag and the difficulty in buying one off the shelf contributed to the exclusivity of the bag. There was a waiting list to get one. Still is, though it's an artificial scarcity I believe. The shops would rather sell the bags to customers who buy other items from Hermès as well, like clothes and scarves. If you are a good customer there is no problem with buying a Birkin or a Kelly but it will cost you."

"Why exactly are they so much more expensive than other brands? Why double price to the Chanel bags for example?" Anna asked.

"Because they say that Hermès bags are made exclusively by hand. Every stitch is hand made by highly trained craftsmen in France. They spend several days on each bag; cutting out the pattern, stitching, polishing and buffing. If the bag is not perfect it will be discarded, never sold at a cheaper price. Owning a Hermès Kelly or Birkin bag is actually an investment because you can always sell it for a good price. Look at the auction houses today. Few times a year they have special sales of Hermès bags. There was this Birkin in crocodile with diamonds on the hardware that sold for 380,000 dollars. Crazy prices."

"Oh yes, that is so expensive." Anna quickly converted the U.S. dollars to the Swedish krona in her head. It came to 3 million Swedish kronas. You could buy a house for this money in Sweden.

"And the Louis Vuitton?" Anna asked as they were passing outside the LV store on Rue du Rhône. "What do you think about these bags princess?" Anna had seen several LV handbags in Sweden. They were very popular there, especially the Monogram range.

"Louis Vuitton is good for luggage, not for handbags. By luggage I mean the smaller cabin bags. Never put a Vuitton suitcase on a commercial flight."

"Why is that?" Anna wanted to know.

"Because they attract too much attention with the handlers. They assume that if people can afford expensive bags, inside the bag must be something expensive as well. Things might disappear from these bags. I only use my Vuitton suitcases when I travel by car or take a private jet, not otherwise."

"But why not handbags?" Anna asked.

"Because there are so many copies out there that the LV logo is not exclusive anymore. They do other styles in leather, mind you, the Monogram and Damier are not leather but canvas, but these leather bags are not classic. They don't stay fashionable like the Chanel or Hermès bags do. Hermès is the Rolls Royce of bags as there is nothing better than that. Chanel comes second but not all models, only the classic flap bag that has looked the same for decades. I have seen many young women carrying the Chanel Boy bag lately as it seems to be very popular. Unfortunately this bag doesn't look like a classic to me. I think that in a few years this bag will be out of fashion meanwhile the flap bag will still be going strong. So put your money into the classics, it's a great investment."

If you have that kind of money, Anna thought. For most people these bags were out of their range. Anna wouldn't mind to carry a Louis Vuitton Speedy bag, she liked it very much. It must be nice to be rich and never think about how much things cost, just buy anything you fancy. The princess was wealthy but she didn't overspend, on the contrary, she made her purchases with careful consideration. By buying high quality classic items, the princess always looked elegant, never outdated and her items lasted many years.

Anna saw her wardrobe that evening when the princess showed her the red sole shoes by Charles Jourdan. Her dressing room was the size of Anna's living room. It looked like a beautiful shop with Chanel jackets, suits and dresses; all covered in plastic protection bags to keep away dust and mites. There was one wall with what looked like hundreds of shoes. Another one with handbags and several piles of orange Hermès boxes containing Birkin and Kelly bags. The boxes had photographs attached to them so it was easy to see which bag was inside each box. Same for the shoe boxes, a picture on each one, impeccable order everywhere. There were several long ball gowns hanging in another closet. These dresses were truly exclusive, some of them heavily beaded and some almost transparent. Anna was surprised that the princess would wear something that revealing but she didn't say a word. Naturally, there was nothing there from H&M or Zara, not even one item, only expensive brands.

"This is very nice," Anna commented on the closet.

"Thank you Anna. The problem is that I have to stay slim all my life otherwise my clothes won't fit me. It's hard when you are my age."

The thought of wearing the same clothes for decades didn't appeal to Anna, it sounded boring, but each to their own.

"Why don't you chose a dress for dinner and remind me tomorrow morning that we need to go shopping for clothes, after your visit to the hospital that is. Henri must be so happy to see you every day."

"Tomorrow we should have the test results," Anna responded. Thinking of that made her nervous. The princess noticed that it bothered her.

"How exciting," she said. "Are you nervous?"

"Yes, very much. I don't know what I will do if the test is negative. Probably go home the same afternoon."

"Oh, no, there is no need for that my dear. You can stay here as long as you wish. I like you being here with me." Anna reminded the princess of Alexandra, her little baby angel. The daughter she had lost over half-century ago.

"Thank you for saying that, it means a lot to me," Anna said thinking of her mom. She really missed her.

The dinner was served as usual at eight o'clock. The princess entered the dining room wearing a long evening dress and a diamond necklace. She carried Coco on her arm. Anna picked out a silver Versace gown for herself. She decided to wear her new beige Louboutin shoes together with the dress. It was not a perfect match but she was happy nevertheless. She felt like a princess.

After a glass of wine Anna summoned her courage to ask a question: "How did you learn to be this perfect? Or were you born like this?"

"What do you mean?" The princess asked not entirely sure if this was a compliment or not.

"The way you talk, walk and behave. You are so eloquent. A true lady."

"I see what you mean. Well, I had a great role model in my mother, she taught me everything I know today. But I also had a French gouvernante who was very strict with me. She drilled me on my posture for several years."

"Your posture?"

"Yes. Every meal we had she told me to imagine that I had a string pulling at my head, straight up to the ceiling. Like someone holding a marionette puppet doll. I used to hunch my back when sitting down and she hated that. 'Your back has to be straight when you sit at the table', she reminded me at each meal. Good posture is everything, she would say."

"What else did she teach you?" Anna wanted to know meanwhile making sure that her back was straight.

"That you have to stand straight up with your shoulders down. And that you have to be confident. It took me several years to reach that goal."

Anna wished that she had the confidence of the princess. She seemed to do everything so effortlessly. And she knew stuff, she knew people, she knew everything. Like a walking human Google.

"What would your governess say about me? That I'm a hopeless case?"

"Ha, ha!" the princess laughed. "She would certainly pull that string again. And teach you how to walk in high heels with three heavy books on your head."

"Books, why?"

"Because that's what we used to do back in the days, to have a good posture. Your head has to be up. That's a sign of self-confidence."

"Anything else?"

"Yes, there is plenty more. How to dress, how to converse, how to eat, how to behave, the whole nine yards."

"Can you teach me some of it?" Anna was eager to learn.

"Yes, of course. Where shall we start?"

"Right now here, how to eat. What do I do wrong?"

"You do nothing wrong my dear, but there are certain rules at the table. For example, you have to be on time. Nobody sits down until the host does. Nobody starts to eat until the host says *bon appétit*. If there are several forks and knifes in front of you then you start from the outside. Your napkin has to be on your lap, not on the table. You toast by raising your glass, never touching someone else's. You hold the glass by its stem, like this," she showed Anna. "Chew slowly and never talk with the food inside your mouth. Put your fork and knife down between the bites, it's not a competition who can finish first. I have seen so many *faux pas* in my life I could write a book about it. There is no education these days so the young people don't know how to behave. So many times when dining in restaurants I have seen people sitting together but they are not present, they are inside their phones. It's not only rude but it's tragic. A meal is about a moment of togetherness, it's special. We need to connect at least once a day so sitting together and sharing food is important. Many people don't have that. They eat in front of the television."

Yes, it's true, Anna related to that as she spent many evenings eating alone on the sofa while watching TV. At least she didn't bring her phone to the dinner table tonight.

"Any other tips on how to be a lady?" Anna asked.

"My mother always told me that you can only make first impression once, so always dress nicely and put your makeup on because you never know whom you might meet that day. Like the ad for American Express in the 1980's – *Don't Leave Home Without It.* Don't leave home without your lipstick. Well, you are young so you don't need the makeup, but an older woman definitely needs some extra help."

So far Anna hasn't seen the princess with a bare face as she was always made up before exiting her bedroom in the morning.

"How you dress is also very important," she continued. "The clothes don't need to be expensive, it's not about that, they should fit you properly, so a good seamstress that can alter them is a must. For example, I always need to shorten my sleeves as my arms are not that long. Same with pants, they never make them the perfect length for me. Small alternations here and there make a huge difference to the overall appearance. A lady needs a good hairdresser, a good beautician and a good seamstress in her life. And a good gynecologist, but that's another story," she chuckled. After a glass of wine she seemed to loosen up a bit.

"So speaking about opening the legs," she was getting naughty now, "one of the difficult things to master is how to get out of a car without flashing anyone. Keep your legs together and turn both legs to the side, just like this," she showed Anna on her chair. "Legs always together."

Anna copied her. Okay, got it.

Rosita brought in the dessert which was *crème brûlée*, the size of a mini cupcake. Anna loved sweets so she wished this treat was bigger. The princess took only two spoons of the dessert and left the rest behind.

"Sweets are not good for you," she said matter of fact.

"So why are we having dessert?" In Sweden people don't have dessert every day, only on special occasions, Anna thought.

"It's a tradition here," the princess answered. "The French cuisine is like that, the dessert completes the meal. Unfortunately it goes straight to your hips. Let's move to the living room and sit on the sofa, it's more comfortable there."

She lifted Coco from her chair and gave the dog to Rosita. "Take her to pee-pee," she said to the maid. Coco's potty and exercise place was at the rooftop terrace. The dog never walked on the street, she traveled only in the Chanel bag. Her tiny poop was dutifully collected by the maid and flushed down the toilet. The grass on which she peed was changed every season. It was immaculate, like a green on a posh golf course.

The two women sat in front of the fire place. Hanging on the wall over the mantel was an oil painting of the princess and her husband.

"How long ago was this?" Anna asked pointing at the painting.

"Few years before he died," said the princess. "He was a good man, my Leopold. I miss him dearly."

"I miss my mom too," Anna said with sadness in her voice.

"Yes, it's sad when people die but we are here now and we have to live, not cry. So let me teach you how to be a lady," she said winking.

"Great, I like that," said Anna. Anything to distract her from tomorrow's test results at the hospital was a good idea.

"So a lady never swears, she is always polite and courteous. The words like *thank you* and *please* are standard behavior. She never raises her voice, shows her emotions in public, or makes a scene. It's better to withdraw in dignity. She never gossips about other people and never talks down to anyone. Gosh, no many *nevers*. She gives compliments and feels comfortable in receiving them as well."

Anna tried to memorize everything. She wished she had a writing pad in front of her.

"The way you dress shows the world who you are so chose your clothes carefully. Don't show too much skin. If the dress is short, cover up your chest and neck otherwise you might look indecent. By short I mean knee length, not short up to here," she pointed at her thigh. "Showing too much cleavage makes you look cheap, not sexy. If you can only afford one dress then buy a good quality black one that will take you anywhere, from lunch to dinner to a party. A string of white pearls is a must, it always looks classy. Shoes have to be of good quality and never scuffed. People notice these things you know. This applies to both men and women."

Anna's white sneakers had seen their better days, she thought. Time to clean them up.

"Speaking of men, shoes are of great importance," the princess continued. "They should always be clean and well polished.

Anna thought of Maxence. Were his shoes clean? She honestly didn't notice as all she could see was his beautiful blue eyes.

"Why are cars important to men?" Anna asked having Maxence in mind.

"Because men will always be boys, however old they get. These cars are their toys. There is also an element of competition there as they like to show off to each other. The bigger, the faster, the costlier, you name it. It's the male ego talking through the steel, or whatever metal they are made of these days. It's their reptilian brain thinking."

"Do you mean to say that they are like reptiles? The men?"

"No my dear, not at all. What I mean is that they use the oldest part of their brain, the one that we share with reptiles, that controls basic functions for survival. It's this brain telling them to compete. The more money they have, the bigger toys they buy. And watches of course. Watches are important to a man. An expensive watch is a status symbol just like the car."

"Is this the reason that every man wants to have a Rolex watch?"

"I guess, however, Rolex here in Geneva is considered a *poor man's watch* as the wealthy people buy Patek Philippe and other more expensive brands. Rolex is mostly sold to tourists. It's still a beautiful watch though, don't get me wrong."

Anna would be delighted to own a Rolex watch. She glanced at the princess' wrist to see what brand she was wearing. It was a yellow gold Cartier Panthère watch, a rather small and discreet piece. She liked the look of it.

"Can I ask you about yesterday's visit to the Kempinski hotel?" Anna said changing the topic. "Why didn't you use the revolving doors?"

"Because I don't like them. Once I saw a little boy in New York trapped inside these doors. He was screaming his lungs out, meanwhile his panicking mother tried to get to him but the door was stuck. Finally the fire brigade came to rescue the poor little boy. Since that day I always take the side door."

Rosita brought back Coco from the terrace.

"Let's have some sleep because tomorrow is a big day for you my dear."

Anna didn't sleep well during the night as millions of thoughts buzzed in her head. When she finally dozed off in the morning hours, she dreamt about a white flying horse with beautiful wings, a white *Pegasus*. She was riding the horse while looking down at the world from high above. She felt invincible.

Upon opening her eyes the panic struck again. Her stomach was churning and it was difficult to breathe. She called Elin.

"Calm down silly, everything will be fine. You survived all your life without him so if he isn't your father, you will be fine."

"How can I recreate the look from yesterday?" Anna wanted to know. "I have this bag here full of makeup but not a clue what to do with it."

"I have an idea," Elin said convincingly. "Go to Annie Jaffrey's channel on YouTube. She has great makeup tutorials that you can follow step by step. It's easy and she is the best."

"Of course, I should have thought of it myself," she answered. They had been watching Annie's channel together and Anna liked her very much. Annie had always been an inspiration for health, positivity and beauty. She had many followers on YouTube and Instagram.

Anna was watching Annie's video when the princess entered the room.

"Are you ready my dear? Maxence will be here shortly."

"Just finishing my makeup. This is so hard to do," she said while applying the eyeliner as the two lines didn't look the same. One was more winged than the other.

"Oh, you are watching Annie. Do you know her?"

the princess sounded surprised.

"She is a Swedish health and beauty guru on YouTube, but she lives in Switzerland, I believe," said Anna. "Do you know her?"

"Actually I do. She is the gorgeous daughter of my psychologist Dr. Bea Jaffrey."

"Really? You have a psychologist? Why?"

"Because everyone needs one. She helped me a lot when my husband died. She is great. Maybe you should see her as well? I can arrange an appointment."

Anna was not keen on talking to psychotherapists but a meeting with Annie would be something else. She had followed Annie since her New York university days. The girl is beautiful both inside and out, and she has a positive energy around her.

Maxence was already downstairs ringing the bell. Let me guess, she thought, he is driving a new car today.

Rightly so, the car of the day was a white Pagani Huayra, another uncomfortable low seated supercar. This one had doors opening up over its roof, the so-called gullwing doors. Oh my God, this is my white Pegasus dream from last night. These doors look like wings and the car is white. How strange.

"You look nice today," he noticed. "What happened to the pony tail?"

She blushed but said nothing about her new haircut. This was too embarrassing as she was not used to compliments from handsome men.

Maxence helped her into the car. The interior was a mixture of carbon-fiber and aluminum, a blend of old looking gauges and new technology. How interesting she thought. She found the dashboard aesthetically pleasing.

"Are you going to tell me the price of this one as well?" she teased. "And the engine of course, I need to know that."

Maxence was not in the mood for jokes today. All he cared about right now was the test result for the bone marrow. Was she willing to be a donor if the test was positive? Would she do that for their dad?

Anna was nervous all the way to the hospital. *You will be fine, you will be fine*, she repeated Elin's words in her head while they approached the hospital.

Doctor Pichou entered Henri's hospital room carrying a bunch of papers.

"Is everyone here? he asked Henri. "Is Mathilda coming?"

"No, she never gets up before eleven so let's start." He didn't want Mathilda to know about Anna so there was no reason for her being here.

"So the results are in and I have some good news to tell you," he started turning his face to Anna. "You Anna Andersson are indeed Henri Duponte's daughter. Congratulations to both of you!"

"Really? I'm so happy," she jumped into the air. Finally she knew who her father was. But was Henri happy as well? He looked very pale and not surprised at all. Suddenly she was confused as doctor Pichou continued to read from the paper.

"The blood test for bone marrow is positive as well. You are a good match Anna," he said looking at her with a smile. "Congratulations."

"What bone marrow? What is that?" she asked, surprised by his statement.

Maxence was up on his feet now.

"Listen Anna, my father needs a bone marrow transplant urgently. He has terminal cancer and you are the only one to save him."

"That's enough Maxence," Henri shouted at his son. "Leave Anna alone. I'm not doing this."

"You have cancer?" Anna asked Henri, her eyes wide. "Why didn't you tell me?"

"Because I didn't want to worry you Anna," said Henri in a calmer voice now. "And I'm not doing any transplant. It's too late. I'm too old."

"Dad, you still have a chance so please do this. Pierre, say something." He turned to the doctor for help.

"Henri, please consider it. The trials have been promising this far. Take a shot at it."

Henri looked at Anna with a tired expression on his face. "No, let me die in peace. I don't want any of this. No chemo, no radiation, rien de rien."

Suddenly, Maxence stormed out of the room leaving Anna alone with the two men. Doctor Pichou excused himself and swiftly left the room as well. A painful silence followed.

They called me here because they wanted my help, nothing else. He doesn't care if I'm his daughter or not, he only needs me to donate something. What did the doctor say? Bone marrow? What is that? And how am I supposed to donate it? Anna had many questions on her mind. The good news of finding her long lost father got trumped by the cancer shock. How long is he going to live? And what shall I do now? I need to talk to the princess urgently.

Anna took a taxi back to the old city. She didn't have the address but knew that the princess' apartment was close to the cathedral. On the way she called her aunt Birgitta in Sweden to tell her what had happened at the hospital.

"Pack your bags and come home quickly," her aunt advised her. "Your mother was right about him, he is just using people."

Upon listening to Anna's story, the worried princess called Henri but was unable to reach him. She also called Maxence who explained the situation to her in detail.

"We need to see a specialist for a second opinion," she decided. Deeply saddened by the news of Henri's cancer and the uncertain prospect of Anna's life saving procedure, she called a friend who knew a world renowned oncologist in the U.S. She would speak to him the same evening.

Anna was surprised by the speed of rich people's actions. Remembering the waiting time it took for her mother's hospital appointments in Sweden, such a quick response was astonishing to her. It seems that knowing people is everything in life. You have to build your networks, she thought.

The telephone consultation with the oncologist confirmed what Anna had already heard that morning. The transplant was a good idea and there was not much risk involved for her except some mild discomfort afterwards.

"My dear," the princess said, "you have to make the decision by yourself. Whatever you chose, I will support you."

8

CANNES, SOUTH OF FRANCE 1991

Henri arrived at the party just after midnight. The iconic Palais Bubbles, a futuristic villa owned by Pierre Cardin was located on the Esterel hill, overlooking the bay of Cannes. It's unusual bubble design and magnificent view over the Mediterranean Sea made the villa the number one place to be seen. The annual Cannes Film Festival rented this place each year for their events.

Henri didn't like parties, he was here for a meeting with the head of a Hollywood movie studio who wanted to invest in European property. He found the fat balding man in the swimming pool, surrounded by several bikini clad young starlets.

"Come, join me in the pool!" the honcho shouted to Henri. "My girls will take care of you," he added with a big grin on his face.

"No, thank you, I will stay here," Henri replied

politely. "I have another meeting in an hour in the city," he lied. This was not what Henri expected while driving up the winding hill to the house. The trip made him sick and the thought of driving back in the middle of the night made him even more anxious. God, I hate these people, he thought. They have money but no class.

He decided to walk over to the bar to get a glass of water. The place was crowded with drunk people, mostly wannabe models, producers and movie stars. Henri made his way across the pool area. There were several waiters carrying trays with champagne glasses but no drinking water in sight. Finally, the barman directed him to the kitchen.

"Good evening," Henri said when entering the busy room. Several caterers were rushing around preparing food trays, no one paying any attention to him. "Can I have some mineral water?" he asked.

"Yes, of course sir," he heard a female voice behind his back. "Fizzy or flat?"

"Flat would be fine, thank you," he said while turning around. To his astonishment he found himself in front of the most beautiful young woman. She was wearing a white blouse, black skirt and black ballerina flats. She was as tall as Henri, looking straight into his eyes. Wow, he thought, what a beauty. She is totally different from the crowd outside. No makeup, blonde hair tied up in a pony tail and those piercing blue eyes looking straight into his soul. He was taken aback by her alluring smile, her innocence, her aura of fresh radiance. She is so young she could be my daughter, he thought with regret.

"I'm Henri," he said while reaching out his right

hand toward her.

"Cecilia," she answered shyly taking his hand, her cheeks blushing.

"So Cecilia, where are you from?" he asked curiously as she didn't look French to him.

"I'm from Sweden. Just here for the summer. I'm studying French during the day and working as a waitress at night," she said with a strong accent. "And you?"

"I'm here for work. I usually live in Geneva but I also have a place here in Cannes," he answered, not able to move his eyes away from her face. She fascinated him. Though he was 50 years old he felt like 20 again. The exhilarating rush of blood, so long ago forgotten, made its presence once again. He felt alive, young, and he was developing an erection.

"Let me show you Cote d'Azur tomorrow," he ventured, trying to seize the moment.

"Oh, I don't know," she answered verily. "I have school in the morning."

"And in the afternoon? Do you have a couple of hours free? We could go to Grasse, to the perfume factory. Have you been there already?"

"No, I haven't," she answered with less hesitation than before. "That would be fun," she added with a smile.

"Great. Let me pick you up tomorrow at two o'clock. Where will you be?"

"At school. Do you know the restaurant le Vesuvio on the Croisette? My school is just behind it but I can meet you in front of the restaurant."

"Yes, I do, but give me your phone number just in case," he said feeling satisfied with himself for progressing so smoothly.

She scribbled down her number on a napkin for him.

"Here you go. And here is your water. See you tomorrow," she said while rushing out off the kitchen.

Henri put the napkin in his pocket, took the water and made his way back to the pool area.

"Henri, Henri! Here you are!" the fat man was shouting from the cabana. He was out of the pool now, wearing a thick bathrobe and smoking a huge Havana cigar, still surrounded by several young women.

"Have a cigar Henri. And any girl that you like. They are all yours," he said with a grin.

What Henri wanted was Cecilia and he was going to have her, no matter what.

At two o'clock sharp, Henri was parked outside the le Vesuvio. He was driving a red Porsche 911 Carrera Cabriolet, a convertible sports car.

Cecilia showed up few minutes late wearing dark sunglasses, white shorts, blue t-shirt and white sneakers. She looked even younger today. Henri greeted her with a kiss on her cheek and off they went toward the mountains.

The next few weeks they spent almost every afternoon together. He took her to places like Monaco and Saint-Tropez. Though he never tried to kiss her on her lips, he showered her with gifts. He told her that he was separated from his wife and that he had a son back home in Geneva. Cecilia was okay with that but she wondered why Henri wouldn't make a move on her. Was there anything wrong with her?

Did he consider her too young for him? She just turned 19 that spring but in her mind she was an adult and certainly not a virgin. And Henri didn't look 50, he was fit and dressed in the latest fashion. For her, the age difference was not a problem. Besides that she liked the attention. It was nice to be wooed by a rich and classy man. He had good manners, something that her previous Swedish boyfriends lacked. He was respected by everyone and wherever they went, people knew his name. Some assumed that Cecilia was his daughter but she was fine with that. They had a few laughs because of it.

When the rumor that Henri was seeing a much younger woman reached Mathilda in Geneva, she was hurt but said nothing. She believed that this was just another fling of his, like so many before. Soon he would be back home with her and the other woman would become history.

August came and they still hadn't had sex. Cecilia became impatient as she was due to return to Sweden in couple of weeks.

"Do you find me sexy," she asked Henri when they were sunbathing on his yacht.

"Of course I do," Henri answered surprised that she would ask such a thing. "You are stunning, you could be a model."

"So why don't you want to make love to me?" she questioned. "What's wrong with me?"

"Nothing is wrong with you Cecilia. It's me. I'm much older than you," he said while looking into her beautiful blue eyes. "I would love to take you in my arms and kiss you. All over your body," he added.

Cecilia reached out to him, took his hand and led him downstairs under deck.

From that day on they would sleep together at his ultra chic and modern apartment on the Croisette, only a block away from the Carlton hotel. She quit her evening job, secretly wishing that Henri would ask her to stay with him. She was in love and she hoped that Henri felt the same about her, though he never mentioned the "L" word. With only a few days left to go, Cecilia ventured to ask the hard question:

"Would you like me to stay here? I could, you know. I could take a sabbatical year at the university and stay here with you. We are good together."

One look at Henri's face said it all. He looked perplexed and not at all happy as she had wished for.

Oh no, she thought. He doesn't love me, he doesn't want me here. She felt devastated.

"I thought that you had to go back to school," he said in a low voice, almost whispering the words. "My project is soon finished here so I will go back to Geneva in a few days."

"I can come with you then, if you want that is," she sounded desperate now, she knew it and she hated herself for that.

"I don't think it's possible right now," Henri answered, carefully measuring his words. Mathilda's face came flashing in front of his eyes. It was one thing to have a mistress in Cannes, but to do the same in Geneva was not feasible. Mathilda would never let it happen and divorces were very expensive. Besides that, it could take several years for a divorce to finalize as Mathilda would make sure to oppose every proposition to settlement. Then it was their 4-year-old son Maxence that Henri hadn't seen all summer. He knew that Mathilda would use the boy as a pawn in the divorce and he wanted to be close to his son. So no, for now it was better for Cecilia to return to Sweden and then he would figure something out. They could see each other in various other places like Paris, New York or London. Henri had to travel, so why not meet there? Did Cecilia want more? It looked like it but she was only 19 for God's sake! What did she know about life?

He looked at her wanting to say something soothing as her eyes were filling with tears, her body shaking uncontrollably. Suddenly she grabbed her handbag and ran towards the door.

"Cecilia!" he shouted after her. "Come back, please," but she was already outside, running down the stairs. He tried to call her, only to hear the ringing of her phone she left behind.

The next morning Mathilda arrived unannounced with Maxence. The boy was very happy to finally see his dad. They went fishing together on Henri's yacht.

Cecilia gathered together all the gifts that Henri had gotten her during the summer; the clothes, shoes, handbags and the jewelry, even the sexy underwear from La Perla. She packed everything carefully in the original boxes, making sure nothing was missing. She changed her flight reservation to that afternoon and booked a taxi to the Nice airport. She asked the driver to make a stop at the Croisette so she could return Henri's gifts and hopefully get back her phone.

The doorman let her in as he knew her by now. She rang the bell on the door, hoping that Henri or his maid would be there. Much to her surprise, an older woman in her 40s answered the door.

"Who are you?" she demanded.

"Who are you?" Cecilia countered.

"I'm Mrs. Duponte, Henri's wife," the woman said sternly, looking her straight in the eyes.

"I thought you were separated, that's what Henri told to me."

"Well, he lied. He always does. You are not the first one and certainly won't be the last one either," Mathilda said, lifting her face to the girl.

Cecilia started to tremble, not being able to utter another word. She pushed the bags inside the entrance, turned around and ran downstairs to the awaiting cab. She cried all the way to the Nice airport.

9

GOTHENBURG, SWEDEN
1991

The university started by the end of August and by that time Cecilia was enrolled in several classes. She was also working at the local coffee shop in the evenings. Though she hated Henri for what he had done to her, she was day dreaming about him, seeing him walking through the door, falling down on one knee and proposing to her with a large diamond ring, just like she had seen in the American movies.

Engagements in Sweden are much different from the Hollywood romances where the couple decides together when and how to get engaged. They buy two plain bands, one for her and one for him, usually in red or white gold. They exchange the rings and put an announcement in the local newspaper. Voila! They are engaged. If and when they get married, they buy another ring for the bride. This is the ring that the groom puts on the bride's finger during the ceremony. This ring can have small diamonds, like an eternity ring or no stones at all. So the wife wears two bands and the husband one. The Hollywood way of engagement with a grand proposal and even grander diamond is the fairy tale that so many women are dreaming about, Cecilia included.

Weeks passed with no sign of Henri. The gloomy Gothenburg weather arrived in early October. From now on it would be cold, wet and dark until spring next year. Cecilia began feeling sick not realizing that she could be pregnant. The thought didn't cross her mind as Henri always used a condom and her periods were irregular anyway. Sometimes it would be a couple of months between the bleedings. It was her mom who told her to go and have a checkup.

By the time she got to the doctor, Cecilia was 12 weeks pregnant. Too late for an abortion she was told, but she could give the baby up for adoption if she wanted. She decided to keep it. Her mom and her aunt Birgitta volunteered to help her. Naturally, they also wanted to know who the father was. She told them but she also made them promise never to contact him to let him know about the baby. She didn't want him in her life complicating things or risking losing the baby to a rich and powerful man. She had read stories about foreign men kidnapping the children from Sweden and hiding them abroad. She didn't want this to happen to her. She could still see Mathilda's arrogant face in front of her. That horrible woman will never touch her baby, ever.

When Anna was born she looked like Henri. His eyes, his nose, his chin, there was no mistake she was his. Not that she had sex with anyone else that summer but the resemblance was amazing. A mini Henri was born, sans the penis.

Cecilia raised Anna alone. It wasn't easy at times but the girl was nice and sweet. She still looked like Henri, with her dark hair and hazel brown eyes, so different from her blonde, blue-eyed mother. Some people would even ask if she was adopted, which annoyed Cecilia. Stupid people, she thought, mind your own business.

Looking at Anna each day reminded her of Henri. She could see his face in her child, his mannerism in her hands and his smile on her lips. His facial expressions were very similar to Anna's. This is crazy, she thought. I love my daughter but I hate her father, yet she reminds me of him, the person that I loathe. How can I live with that? How can I forget what he did to me? Finally, she came to terms with the dilemma, trying to accept Anna for who she was and not for who her father was. She was lucky to have such a loving child. Life was good after all.

10

GENEVA, SWITZERLAND

"**Pierre, what happens** when we die?" Henri asked doctor Pichou.

"What do you mean Henri?"

"You know, in the moment of death, what happens to you? You must have seen so many people dying during your years at the hospital. Or having near death experiences. What do they say when they come back? What about the tunnel and the light?"

"Yes, it's true, some people see a bright light," Pierre responded. "There might be an explanation to that though. When the blood stops flowing, the oxygen supply to the eyes stops as well. This might cause tunnel vision with the bright light on the end of it. What I have noticed is that many people close to death see their dead relatives in front of them. It seems that these relatives come forward to make a smooth transition to the afterlife. If there is such a thing of course. What do you think Henri? Do you believe in life after death?"

"No, I don't," Henri said. "You die and you are gone." Henri didn't believe in God and the idea of heaven or hell was not realistic to him.

"Do people soil themselves after death?" he asked Pierre.

"Some do and some don't," Pierre answered. "If you bladder is full it will leak after death as the urinary sphincter relaxes. Defecation is less common, though it happens sometimes when you move the body and if there is pressure on the stomach. Usually it doesn't happen so don't worry about it."

That was reassuring, Henri thought. He looked down at the urinary drainage bag hanging at the side of his bed. At least I have the catheter so I will not wet the sheets.

"And these relatives?" he asked again. "What if you don't like some of them? Will they still come?"

"Hard to say. I think only the people that you had good connection with in the past come forward. Someone you loved and respected, so you are looking forward to the journey. The people that passed to the other side and then came back describe the transition as a very pleasant and peaceful experience. They would rather stay dead than live here on earth. Their perception of life changes completely. The other side seems so much better, so much happier than here. There seems to be this positive energy that everyone is feeling. We are not allowed to talk about it as many people would commit suicide if they knew how good death feels. I don't understand why people are so scared of death. They shouldn't be. Death is part of life or as my father once said, life is a waiting room for death."

Pierre's father was a doctor as well so he must

have known, Henri thought.

"Yeah, I get what you mean," Henri concurred. "Though death might be good, the people we leave behind suffer a lot." He was thinking about his parents and his brother David, and the anguish they left behind. Who will miss Henri? Maxence for sure and maybe a couple of non relatives like Mike and Clotilde. He knew Mathilda would be fine without him as long as she had plenty of money in her account. And Anna, his new found daughter? Would she miss him? Probably not. The girl was sweet but totally naïve. The Dupontes were big achievers yet she didn't have the Duponte zest for life, the hunger to succeed, the high ambition, the guts to win and to push forward. Just like her mother Cecilia. I wish I could teach her about life but now it's too late, my time is out.

Henri woke up the next morning feeling so much better. Wow, another day and I'm alive, he thought. The sun is shining, life is good. He didn't need his pain medication today, he felt great. Suddenly, by the foot of the bed he saw his father. He was wearing a dark suit, white shirt and a tie, the same clothes he wore at his burial 50 years ago.

"Dad, is that you?" he gasped in disbelief.

Henri senior didn't say a word but the look on his face was the loving one that Henri remembered from his childhood.

"Dad, say something," Henri hoped for a conversation. "Anything."

His father took a step back and now Henri's mother came forward, wearing a long white gown. She stretched her arms toward him, like she was welcoming him into her bosom, the rightful place for a little boy to be.

"Maman!" he said in French. "How are you feeling?"

"I am fine Henri," she answered in a soft voice. "I have been missing you all these years. And look, your brother David is here as well to see you. Can you see him?"

No, Henri could not see David. He wondered if David was still mad at him, therefore not willing to materialize himself in front of Henri. Oh well, never mind, as long as his parents were here, he thought.

Without any effort, Henri stood up from his bed and walked toward his mother. They embraced warmly, her kissing him three times on his cheeks.

"My loving son," she whispered in his ear. "Welcome home."

Maxence entered the hospital room to see his father sleeping peacefully in his bed. Suddenly the monitor behind him flat-lined, automatically starting the alarm. Maxence shouted out for help but it was too late, they couldn't revive his father. Henri Duponte junior was gone.

Upon hearing the sad news from Maxence, Anna and the princess rushed to the hospital to bid their final farewell to Henri. Both women cried. One had just lost a longtime dear friend and the other one a newly found father.

Though Anna's leave of absence from work was over, she decided to stay for the funeral. She called her boss and begged for understanding as her father just passed away in Switzerland. The news spread quickly at the office because by three o'clock that afternoon she received a text from Christer, her two timing ex. He said he missed her and that she was the love of his life. No mention about her father, as if he didn't know but Anna was sure he did, which was the reason he got in touch with her in the first place. What did he want from her now? Jerk. She blocked him without replying.

The princess was grateful to have Anna stay longer. They would chat several times a day. Anna wanted to know more about her father and the princess willingly complied. She had known Henri all her life.

"He was a good man," she said to Anna. "Leopold always said that Henri was loyal to him."

They were sitting in front of the fireplace when the princess asked Anna, "I need a huge favor from you my dear. Can you please help me with a very important mission?"

"Yes, of course," she said eager to help. "What is it? What can I do for you?"

"You see that golden urn on the mantel," she pointed toward the fireplace, "that's my Leopold. Before he died I promised him I would scatter his ashes at his favorite places. That was five years ago and I have been postponing it since then because I wanted him close to me. But no one lives forever so now is the time to fulfill his wish. The problem is that I can't do it alone, I need your help. Will you be my partner in crime?" she asked.

"Why do you say *crime*? Is it illegal?" Anna wanted to know.

"Let's say it's borderline illegal as you have to ask

for permission and I don't want to take the risk of a rejection because I will do it anyhow. But with your help it will be easier."

"So what are we going to do? Where did he want to spread them?"

"There are three places that meant a lot to him; Lake Geneva, because we met here; Monte-Carlo, because we went there for our honeymoon, and Dubai, because that was our last trip together. So the plan is that we start with the lake and then fly to Monaco, then to Dubai and back to Geneva. Have you been to these places before?"

"No, never." Anna didn't travel much except for charter vacations to Spain or Greece. "We didn't go further than Europe with my mom, it was too expensive. Before she died we spoke about going to Fiji as it sounded so exotic. Fidji was the name of her favorite perfume."

"Oh, I know that perfume, it's by Guy Laroche. It was very popular in the 70's and early 80's. They discontinued the production for a couple of years and then relaunched it because women were protesting. The new formula was slightly different from the original one. Still a beautiful scent though."

Yes, Fiji had been on her mother's bucket list forever. Unfortunately she didn't live long enough to go there.

The prospect of traveling with the princess excited Anna. "How many days will the trip take? I have to go back to work you know."

"We should be back within a week or so. And speaking of work, maybe you shouldn't worry so much about it. I'm sure Henri left something for you in his will. He was a wealthy man you know."

"I think it's awkward to ask Maxence or his mother for money, don't you think?" Anna said. Besides, she didn't want anything from them. She had offered to help Henri with the bone marrow transplant but he refused. What else could she do? Maxence was furious with her because it took her two whole days to decide whether she would do it or not. He blamed her for his father's death, or at least she thought he did since he didn't answer her calls and the funeral was nearing.

"This is not how you do it, you don't ask for money. We have to call my lawyer and see what he can do," the princess said.

Anna went to the funeral with the princess. They were both wearing black dresses, white pearls and black Kelly bags. The princess graciously offered Anna to choose any bag from her collection.

The church was full when they arrived. The paparazzi tried to take pictures in front of the entrance but were pushed away by security guards. This was much different from her mother's quiet funeral a few months ago.

After the service Maxence spotted Anna in the crowd and made his way over to her.

"What are you doing here?" he said angrily. How dare you to come here?"

"He was my father too you know. Why shouldn't I be here?" She tried to stay calm but was shaking inside.

"Really? You can't prove that. You should go back to Sweden where you belong. You are not welcome here."

114

"What do you mean? You were there when the test results came in. You know he was my father too, don't you?" She was boiling now.

"You should have tried to convince him about the transplant. Make him do it. But you did nothing! If you think you will get some money from us you are mistaken." His face was close to hers and she could feel his breath on her skin. "Not a centime, bitch! Get lost! I never want to see you again!" He turned around and disappeared into the crowd.

On the way back home Anna, who was still upset, told the princess what had happened.

"He is not himself right now, he is mourning his father. I'm sure he didn't mean it," the princess said. She always had kind words to say about other people, how did she do it? Anna had never heard her complain or gossip about others. Such a remarkable woman she was, always full of energy and positivity.

A few days later they were summoned to the lawyer's office. Maître Haville didn't have good news. Henri's will didn't include Anna as it was drawn few years ago, before he knew she existed. Furthermore, there was no record of her blood test in the hospital. The lawyer tried to contact doctor Pichou but unfortunately he was retired and couldn't be reached. Mathilda and Maxence Duponte didn't want to have anything to do with Anna and referred her to their lawyer. His advice was to sue them but it would take a long time and cost thousands of Swiss francs.

"Don't worry," said the princess, "we will figure something out. We have a trip to plan first."

The secret mission started the next day. When Rosita went out shopping, the two women carried the heavy golden urn to the kitchen. Leopold's ashes were divided in three equal piles and neatly tucked inside zipped bags.

Their first stop was Lake Geneva, a short walk from the apartment. The princess wanted to scatter the ashes close to the fountain. The problem was that the place was crowded with tourists.

"We have to come during the night, the princess said. When no one is here. Desperate measures call for desperate actions."

That night, they dressed in black sports clothes and jogging shoes. Full of excitement, like two thieves planning a heist, they discussed the best approach to scatter the ashes without being noticed. Anna would pretend to tie her shoe laces, meanwhile the princess and Coco were on the lookout. When down on the ground she would open the zip lock bag and empty the ashes over the water.

The dumping of the ashes went according to the plan. They stayed a few more minutes to say prays and then went back home.

"First mission accomplished," said the contented princess. Now they had to pack for Monte-Carlo and Dubai.

The next day they went to Bongénie, the exclusive department store for branded clothes. The shop was only a few minutes' walk from the Cathedral.

"You need to buy some beach wear my dear," the princess said to Anna. "Swimsuits, bikinis, pareos, beach sandals and summer dresses. It's very hot in

Dubai during the summer."

Anna picked up a few items, daring not to look at the price tags, knowing things would be expensive here. With the princess' help she managed to put together a few outfits.

"Which one do you prefer?" she asked the princess as it was hard to choose between them.

"We will take them all and if you don't like something we can always bring it back to the store. No problem."

This is a nice way to shop, Anna thought. Just pick out anything you like and bring back the stuff that you didn't use on the vacation. This was new to her.

Back home they prepared for the trip. The princess had a packing list to follow so she ticked off everything that went into her suitcase. How practical, Anna thought. She is so organized, unlike Anna who used to forget things.

"What time is the flight tonight?" Anna wanted to know.

"We have a slot at seven."

"Slot? What is that?"

"It's the time for take-off."

At six o'clock a black limousine was waiting downstairs to take them to the airport. Though Anna was excited about the trip, the princess had a sad expression on her face. She was almost in tears because Coco had to stay at home with Rosita.

"Sorry my sweet Coco," she said while kissing her, "Mama has to go away for few days but she will be back before you know it."

"Coco can't come with us?" Anna was surprised as

the dog went everywhere with the princess.

"Unfortunately, the hotel in Dubai doesn't allow pets so she has to stay at home this time." She seemed distressed. It must have been very painful to leave the dog behind.

Rosita took Coco from her and bid them farewell:

"Bon voyage princess. Bon voyage Anna. See you soon."

The ride to the airport took them 20 minutes. Anna was surprised when they continued past the main terminal to the other side of the airport. They stopped in front of a smaller building with the sign *TAG Aviation* on. A young man dressed in a black suit jumped into the passenger seat.

"Good evening princess, how are you today? The captain awaits you. We are just on time."

They passed the security guard at the gate and drove into the tarmac where a white Gulfstream G450 was waiting for them.

Anna couldn't believe her eyes. Were they flying by a private jet? How cool is that?

"Is this your plane?" she asked the princess in disbelief.

"Oh, no, I just use it when I need to and they send me the bill afterwards. Nobody owns their planes anymore, they just rent them as it's too much hassle with maintenance and the crew."

The captain and his crew welcomed them onboard. Inside the cabin there were four large beige leather seats in front and another four in the back. At the rear, next to the toilet, there were two three-seat sofas.

"Wow, all this just for the two of us?" Anna was

truly impressed. This was her first time on a private jet. "This is awesome!"

"So nice of you to appreciate it," said the princess, a smile spread across her face. "I'm old now so flying commercial is exhausting to me."

"You are not that old princess," Anna wanted to consol her. "Age is just a number," she had heard that expression many times.

"Yes, my number is a big one my dear. After our mission I don't want to travel anymore." There was a sadness in her eyes that Anna hadn't seen before. Her mouth seemed to drop as she lowered her face. Was she thinking about her late husband? In a way he was here with her, on the bottom of her crocodile Birkin bag. He travelled in style. It must be difficult for her after being married for over 50 years and now he was gone from her life. She must be missing him immensely, just as Anna was missing her mom.

"Let's have a glass of champagne," the princess proposed.

11

MONTE-CARLO, MONACO

The flight to Nice Côte d'Azur International Airport took one hour, just long enough to have dinner and dessert onboard. At arrival they were ushered to the helicopter from Heli Air Monaco.

"Are you okay with helicopters?" the princess asked Anna. "It's only a seven minutes ride compared to half an hour on winding roads. And the view is much better."

"Sure, no problem," she muttered, being much too busy taking selfies with the chopper behind her. Wait until Elin sees this, she thought.

The helicopter ride to Monaco was noisy so they couldn't talk much. Anna was astonished by the view.

"Wow!" she exclaimed. "This is beautiful!"

"Yes, I never get tired of this view," the princess said smiling.

After landing, a limousine was waiting to whisk them to the city center.

"What is the difference between Monaco and Monte-Carlo?" Anna asked. She had heard both names interchangeably but was confused about their meaning.

"Monaco is the country, the principality, and Monte-Carlo is the center of it, the area with the Casino and Hôtel de Paris. I'll show you the hotel tonight. There are different parts of Monaco. Right now we landed in Fontvieille, the newest area with reclaimed land from the sea. All this was water before. The part on the hill over there," she pointed toward the rock, "is Monaco-Ville, the old city with the palace and the cathedral."

Anna was amazed how beautiful this place was.

"A sunny place for shady people, who said that?" she asked the princess. She read it somewhere in the past.

"Somerset Maugham, but he meant the Riviera and not only Monaco. He has been misquoted. He wrote that in his autobiography *Strictly Personal*," she said, an authority on almost everything.

"Why are the rich people coming here? What's so special about Monaco?" The saying *Birds of a feather flock together,* came to her mind.

"Because there is no income or capital tax here. Wealthy people don't want to pay high taxes. Beside that, the climate here is so much better than in the rest of Europe. And the food is good too."

"So can anyone move here?"

"I guess so but to live here is not cheap, Monaco has the highest real estate prices in the world. A small apartment can cost millions."

The car stopped in front of a building on Avenue Princesse Grace, the seafront street known for being the most expensive one on earth. To buy property here may cost up to 100,000 dollars per square meter.

The uniform clad driver helped them take the luggage to the top floor of the building. The princess tipped him and said good night.

"This place is so beautiful. I love the smell of the Mediterranean sea." Anna went to the terrace to look at the view. On her right she could see the port Hercules with its fantastic mega yachts. Above it, on the hill was the palace, standing above the city in its glory, wonderfully lit by hundreds of light beams.

"Have you been to the palace?" she was excited to know. "It must be a fairy tale to live there."

"Yes, of course. Last time was when I was invited to the wedding. It was a marvelous reception. And now they have gorgeous twins, they must be over the moon."

Anna noticed that this apartment was much smaller than the one in Geneva, with only four bedrooms, which by Monaco standards was huge anyhow.

"My dear, I'm truly sorry that we can't stay here longer, because tomorrow we are flying to Dubai," the princess sounded concerned. "We are here on a mission and tonight we are going to Hôtel de Paris. Leopold wanted a part his ashes inside the hotel."

"Why? What's so special about this hotel?"

"In 1961 we came here on our honeymoon. Before we bought this flat we used to stay there each summer. So many memories…" she went quiet as she looked out of the window. "Winston Churchill used to stay there, and Frank Sinatra, and Roger Moore was regular as well. Those were the days."

Who is Winston Churchill again? And Sinatra was

a singer, right? I have to Google them later. Anna felt stupid for not knowing these people but then again she was sure that the princess didn't know who Miley Cyrus was either.

"One summer when they were building the underground garage just outside the hotel," the princess continued, "drilling and hammering all day long, we decided to buy our own place so we ended up here."

"Why don't you live here permanently?" Anna asked. If it was up to her she would be staying here all year long.

"Monaco is not what it used to be. Too many nouveau riche with no class or style."

"Nouveau riche? What is that?"

"New money or newly acquired riches so to say. People that have money but no taste or education. Unfortunately, this is the case for Geneva as well."

Anna wondered if there was an expression for old money in French. Anyhow, she didn't have any money to her name so why bother about it?

"So where did he want the ashes to be placed?" Anna was not sure how they would pull off spreading the ashes *inside* the hotel without being arrested. After all, Monte-Carlo was known for high security measures, having surveillance cameras on every corner, and over 500 police officers watching the city around the clock; according to Elin who had been there before with Stefan. He had taken her to the Monte-Carlo rally earlier this year.

"Reconnaissance first. We have to go there and see how it looks now because they just renovated the hotel. Let's have a drink in the lobby to see what the best action plan would be. Put on comfortable shoes so we can walk there. It's only a ten minute walk but it's mostly uphill so don't wear your Louboutins," she said with a smile. "We need some fresh air, it will do us good."

The streets were lined with exclusive cars all the way to Place du Casino. Café de Paris, the world renowned brasserie next to the Casino was packed with tourists speaking in several languages. People-watching must be so fun here, Anna thought. She could smell the scent of expensive perfumes, or was it the flowers in the middle of the square?

In front of them was a large building with the sign *Hotel de Paris*. They walked up the stairs to the heavy revolving door. Anna remembered that the princess didn't like revolving doors, and rightly so, she went to the side glass door and opened it.

"This is nice," the princess said once they were inside. "They did a great job renovating this place. Oh, and I see the bronze horse statue of Louis XIV is still here. Do you see the right leg of the horse here? Do you know why it looks so worn?"

"No idea."

"Because this is a lucky horse for the Casino players. Before going next door to gamble, the tradition is to rub the horse's leg for good luck. Leopold used to do that. He must have touched this leg a hundred of times."

"So was he lucky then? Did he win a lot?" Anna asked.

"Not really, but that's another story. Let's see where we can have a drink."

The spacious lobby of the 150 year-old hotel was beautifully decorated. Anna looked up to the ceiling in the middle of the room. It had an ornate crystal chandelier hanging from the colorful glass dome. The gilded marble colonnades, the frescoes, the exquisite marble floor with the largest carpet Anna had ever seen, made this hotel lobby a magical place. Surveillance cameras were strategically placed throughout the room, covering every angle of it. So what was the plan this time?

They sat down on a beige sofa by the end of the room. The princess ordered two glasses of Dom Pérignon champagne.

"Look at the flower pot over there, the one with the small palm tree," the princess said to Anna, "that's a perfect place to put the ashes inside the earth. What do you think?"

"Actually, that's a great idea, to put them in the earth," Anna responded, relieved that she didn't have to spill the ashes over the fancy carpet. "But how shall we do this without being noticed? There are cameras everywhere."

"If you go to the ladies room and leave me alone here, I can pretend that I am fainting to attract the attention from the waiters. On your way back, go straight to the flower pot and while the people here are focused on me, empty the zip lock bag inside the pot. What do you think?"

"It sounds like a good plan to me but surely the security guards watching the cameras will see me doing something strange, even if the people here might not notice."

"That's a risk we have to take. I will faint when I

see you coming toward the plant. The cameras should zoom in on me and leave you out of sight. Are you willing to take that risk?"

"Yes, let's do it." She must have loved her husband very much to do this for him, Anna thought. She wished that one day she would be in love as well.

Anna gulped the rest of her champagne for more courage and went to the toilet. She was nervous at the idea of spending the night in jail. She unzipped the bag so she could quickly empty it into the pot. She felt a little tipsy after the champagne, not being used to drinking alcohol; and this was the second time today! "Put yourself together, everything will be fine," she said to herself.

The princess waited for Anna's cue. The moment she saw her next to the plant, she called the waiter over.

"Excuse me," she said, "I'm not feeling well." Then she dropped down on the sofa, eyes closed, arms dramatically spread out.

Great, Anna thought. The sofa is soft so she didn't hurt herself. Smart lady.

The waiter panicked and called over his colleagues for help. Suddenly, several people surrounded the princess, trying to revive her. Anna quickly emptied the bag then tucked it into her handbag and ran toward the sofa.

"Grandma! Are you okay? What happened?" she asked the waiter.

"Madame just fainted," the waiter replied, eyes wide.

The princess opened her eyes, sat up straight and smiled to Anna.

"There you are my dear. Let's go home, I'm tired."

"That's okay," Anna said to the waiter. "This happens all the time. She needs her medication. Can we have the check quickly?"

"Yes, of course, Madame," the waiter said relieved that everything was back to normal again.

"Second mission accomplished," said the pleased princess once they were outside. Next stop Dubai.

They were back at the apartment.

"You were fantastic, you could be an actress," Anna said of the princess' performance.

"I would do anything for my Leopold. I loved him dearly."

"I hope I marry a nice man one day. So far in my life I've only met idiots," Anna said. "Why are relationships so difficult?"

"Marriage is not easy. It's a constant compromise. I think people used to be more committed. Back in the day, marriage was for life. Nowadays everyone is getting divorced instead of working things out. They are looking for a new partner, not realizing that after the initial short-lived period of passion, things will be the same as before. You have to work on it. Life is not a Hollywood movie."

"But what if he cheats or is abusive?"

"Then you have to leave of course. You should never tolerate that. Before, women didn't have a choice, they were stuck in the marriage, totally dependent on their husbands. It's different now, so always make sure you have your own money. Be as independent as possible. They will respect you for that."

"When choosing a husband, what should I look for?"

"Make a wish list with the most important things you need in a man. If you check off at least 80% of the boxes, then he is a good match I would say. You will never find a 100% person, they don't exist, so you settle for the 80 and work on the rest. Most women think that once they marry, she'll change the husband. The truth is that these women get disappointed because people don't change easily. They can pretend for a while but in the long run, their true colors emerge. So be honest with each other *before* you get married."

Anna thought of her own mother who had a string of boyfriends but never married. Was it because of her? Was she protecting her daughter? Or was it difficult to find the right guy?

"My mother used to say that to be happily married the man has to love you more than you love him," the princess continued, "but this is an old fashioned way to look at it. I think that as long as you have the same life goals and good sense of humor and can laugh together, you will be fine. And never lose the respect for each other because if you do, then it's only downhill from there. The purpose of life is to be happy, so make each other happy."

"Happiness," Anna said, "how can I be happy when both my parents just died?"

"No one ever dies. Their body might be dead but their energy is still here with us. I'm sure your mom is looking out for you. Henri as well."

"So they are here with us in this room right now?

Do you really believe that?" Anna blurted.

"Yes, I do. My Leopold as well. And my parents. Not only in this room but everywhere. The departed are pure positive energy that surrounds us."

"But if they are here, can we talk to them? Will they answer?"

"You can talk to them or you can communicate through thoughts, it doesn't matter. It's not the language you speak but the vibration you send out. All thoughts are vibrations of the brain. This is what they pick up from you and what you pick up from them."

Wow, this was getting too complicated for Anna. The prospect of communicating with her mother appealed to her of course but the flipside could be that other people would consider her crazy.

As it was already past eleven at night, the princess prepared for bed.

"Tomorrow will be another long day my dear. Get some sleep now. Goodnight."

"Bye, bye, Monaco, hope to see you again soon." They were back in the helicopter on the way to the Nice airport.

"Are we flying private again?" Anna hoped this was the case as she really liked the experience of yesterday.

"Yes, we are. The same plane as yesterday."

Great! She was happy. Isn't it strange how quickly you get used to the good stuff? She didn't mind to travel like this to the end of her life.

"Tell me something unusual about Sweden," the princess said to Anna once they were airborne.

"Something that many people don't know."

"Okay, let me see..." She paused before coming up with something.

"The worldwide chain of H&M stores originates in Sweden. When I was little these shops were called Hennes&Mauritz. Hennes means *hers* in Swedish. From the beginning the store was called Hennes only and sold female garments. Then the founder Erling Persson bought another clothing store called Mauritz Widforss and combined the two first names to one, thus making it a store for both men and women. His son, Stefan Persson, still runs the company today. He is a billionaire."

"Yes, I know," the princess said. "I met him a few times in Stockholm at the Nobel dinner. He is a good looking man." There was a hint of blush on her cheeks. Was it the champagne or was she embarrassed to find a man handsome? Stefan must be in his late 60s, an age that Anna doesn't find *handsome.*

"Speaking of older men," Anna continued, "there is the founder of IKEA, Ingvar Kamprad, who is one of the world's wealthiest people."

"Yes, when he lived in Switzerland, until recently, he was regarded as the richest man in the country," the princess said. "I think he moved back to Sweden after his wife Margaretha died."

"And what about Switzerland?" Anna was curious to learn something new.

"One thing that many people might not know is that the Swiss men keep their military guns at home. This is a long tradition despite the country being neutral and not participating in any wars in the last 500 years. The military service is mandatory for all

Swiss men but women can serve on voluntary basis if they want to. These men go through basic military training when they are 19 years-old and then return to the army each year for a boot-camp, a sort of refresher course so they don't forget their skills. This is one of the reasons they keep their guns at home, to be prepared in case of an invasion. They also have shooting ranges in each village. Shooting either for sport or hunting is very popular in Switzerland and it's easy to get a gun license."

"So there are guns in every home? How come there are no shootings like in the U.S.?" Anna wanted to know.

"This is a good question. Personally I think that the shootings in the U.S. are committed by mentally ill people that unfortunately somehow have access to guns. In Switzerland only 16 homicides with a firearm were reported in 2016, none of these with a military gun. And when it comes to suicide, 20% of people use a gun."

Death and suicide is not something that Anna wanted to talk about.

"What is Switzerland most known for?" She tried to change the subject.

"First of all I would say watches. For example Rolex and Patek Philippe are produced in Geneva. Then chocolate, cheese, cows and cow bells. The Swiss Army Knife, the Red Cross, the banks and the low taxes. The Swiss Alps and skiing. And of course the punctuality of the Swiss trains. And the fact that so many people confuse Switzerland with Sweden. Both countries value their neutrality and neither is getting involved in wars."

"Why are there so many banks there?" Anna

wanted to know.

"Swiss banks are known for their secrecy rules, therefore people from all over the world bring their money there to avoid taxes in their own countries. So-called numbered accounts are standard in private banking. You must have seen this in the movies when a large amount of money is transferred to a secret Swiss account. However, this is not entirely true because the procedure to open a numbered account is exactly the same as for the regular accounts. You have to be present at the bank and show your passport."

"So what's the difference between a numbered account and a regular one?" inquired Anna.

"The amount of confidentiality and privacy I would say. Not all employees of the bank have access to the details of the numbered account holders. These people are more *protected* so to say. But by the end of the day they are all the same, as the secrecy rules cover all clients. There have been some changes though in recent years because of the scandal with American tax evaders. A whistle blower at UBS, the largest Swiss bank, gave a list of their American clients to the U.S. authorities. The bank had to pay 780 million dollars in penalty to the U.S. government. The whistle blower got 104 million dollars for himself as a reward. Since then, American clients are not welcome in Swiss banks and it's impossible for a person with American passport or even a green card to open an account there now. They are *persona non grata*. The law changed as well in regards to European clients, as Switzerland signed an agreement with the European Union so from January 2018, there will be no more bank secrecy between the countries."

"Why are taxes so much lower there than in Sweden?" Anna asked. She had read about wealthy people moving to Switzerland to avoid taxes.

"This is one of the misconceptions that people have about Switzerland as taxes there are low only for wealthy people and big corporations. People on regular salaries pay almost the same tax there as in other European countries. If you take into account the compulsory health insurance that is quite expensive and the high living cost, there is not much left by the end of the month. It's a myth that we have low taxes. The rich benefit of course because they pay less than elsewhere but because they have so much money the tax cut is a good contribution to the Swiss economy. When attracting the big corporations to Switzerland by offering them low taxes, thousands of jobs are created within Switzerland. It's a give and take scenario that works very well. Do you pay high taxes in Sweden?" the princess asked Anna.

"Well, I don't earn very much and I only work half time so no, not that much," Anna responded.

"Why only half time?"

"Because when my mom was sick I needed to take care of her. The government paid me some money to do that, not much, more like a symbolic sum. When she passed I went back to full time at Volvo but because she left me a small pension, the tax on my income was higher. To make the story short, I make more money by working part time and taking the pension, than working full time. The more I work, the more taxes I pay. Does it make sense?"

"Yes, it does, but let's talk about something pleasant now. Cheers!" the princess raised her glass and toasted with Anna.

"So tell me about Dubai. Why are we going there?"

"I love Dubai, it was my husband's favorite place. Leopold was always interested in architecture so he followed several developments there. You know, the first time we went there, there was nothing more than a few houses and plenty of sand. Look at the city now, it's stunning."

Anna had seen pictures of the Dubai skyline before. There was one in particular that caught her attention; the one with clouds below the tall buildings. How fascinating! She couldn't wait to get there.

12

DUBAI, UNITED ARAB EMIRATES

After a seven hour flight from the Nice airport, the private jet landed in Dubai. Anna was super excited as it was her first visit outside of Europe.

The female flight attendant opened the door and wished them goodbye.

Anna stepped out from the plane onto the stairs and almost fainted.

"Wow! This is hot, like stepping into a Swedish sauna." She quickly checked the weather app on her phone to see how many degrees the local temperature was. It showed 40 degrees Celsius. Really? I hope that they have air conditioning in the hotel, she thought.

A black Mercedes waited at the tarmac to take them to the special arrival hall for private jets. They were ushered to a modern air-conditioned room to relax and have a drink meanwhile their passports were being checked by the authorities.

Anna noticed that there were only men working, not one woman in sight. The men didn't wear uniforms but the local white caftan looking robes called Dishdash, and open sandals. They also wore a red and white checkered headscarf, the Guthra, tied with a black rope called the Egal. Who can wear a suit in this heat? she thought.

The princess looked tired. Anna was surprised that at her age she was still willing to travel. She imagined that after 80, one would rather stay at home in front of the television, knitting a sweater or something for your grandchild, but this lady was still going strong.

"Have some tea my dear, it will take at least 15 minutes before they come back with our passports," the princess said.

"Okay, then I will Google Dubai to learn more about the city."

The princess liked Anna's enthusiasm. Clever girl she thought, always willing to learn new things, just like Henri did.

"So here is what Google says," Anna read out load to the princess, "Dubai is a city and emirate in the United Arab Emirates known for luxury shopping, ultramodern architecture and a lively nightlife scene. Burj Khalifa, an 830 meter tall tower, dominates the skyscraper-filled skyline. At its foot lies Dubai Fountain, with jets and lights choreographed to music. On artificial islands just offshore is Atlantis, The Palm, a resort with water and marine-animal parks. Population of Dubai is 2.8 million."

"Are we going to stay there? At the Atlantis?" she

wanted to know as the hotel and the island looked spectacular.

"No, my dear, we are going to another hotel."

"The climate," Anna continued, "Dubai has an arid sub-tropical climate with very hot, humid summer weather averaging 42 degrees (108F) in the daytime and 28 (84F) at night. This is crazy hot, isn't it?"

"Yes, but only in the summer. Rest of the year is quite pleasant, it can even be cold in December-January," the princess answered.

"Here are some more interesting facts that I found: the police in Dubai has a few Ferraris, Lamborghinis and one Aston Martin in their fleet, look here," Anna showed the princess a picture on her phone. "How cool is that? These police officers are so lucky. Oh, and there is zero crime here so they have all the time in the world to drive these nice sports cars without a worry on their minds."

"Only 17% are Emiratis, the rest are foreigners living here. Dubai has the largest indoor mall on the planet, the biggest aquarium, the tallest hotel and the grandest indoor ski park. Really? Ski park? Can we visit all these places?" Anna begged the princess.

"Sorry my dear, not this time, we will only stay for two nights. I need to get back home. But I'm sure you will come back one day and stay much longer."

Bummer, Anna thought. Then she remembered that the only reason they were here was for Leopold and his ashes.

Their passports were back.

"Please follow me," the robed man said escorting

them to the waiting car outside. Anna couldn't believe her eyes when she saw her ride; a white Rolls Royce Phantom.

"Is this your car princess?" she asked in disbelief.

"No, it belongs to the hotel. They sent it for us."

Ok girl, stop drooling, she thought. This was so much better and more comfortable than Maxence's sports cars. This was a classy ride indeed.

The driver named Farook chatted with the princess like as if he'd known her for ages.

"We missed you Madame, five years is too long you know."

"Yes Farook, but after my husband passed away I was not keen on traveling. It's nice to be back though."

The traffic was heavy in this busy city but it flowed nicely nevertheless, so within 30 minutes they reached their destination.

"This is Jumeirah beach, the princess said. "Here on the right is the Wild Wadi water park and here in front of us, over this bridge, is our hotel."

"Really, is this where we are going to stay?" She had seen this hotel hundreds of times on the internet. The Burj al Arab, the most exclusive hotel in the world, the only seven star hotel on the planet. This is unreal, I must be dreaming.

When their car pulled up to the entrance, Anna saw several more white Phantoms lined up in front of the hotel. She wanted to take pictures but felt it might be inappropriate. Maybe tomorrow I can come here and take selfies, she thought.

The general manager of the hotel was waiting outside to greet them, behind him an entourage of employees carrying welcome drinks and wet, cold wash cloths.

"Princess Sobieski, welcome back to Burj al Arab. It's a pleasure to see you again."

Anna followed the princess into the hotel through the side door, omitting the revolving doors again. What is it with these luxury hotels? They always have these doors, she thought.

Once inside, Anna couldn't quit staring in awe. In front of her was a two story cascade waterfall with dancing fountains flanked by two escalators and giant fish tanks on each side of the lobby. The inside atrium of the hotel was so high she got dizzy when looking up to the top.

"Oh my God, this is incredible!" she was overwhelmed with the opulence of this place. The atrium had a colorful honey comb design supported by massive golden pillars that stretched several floors up. Another fountain on the upper lobby level with mosaic glass and dancing streams had a center water jet that shot up to the roof with lightning speed.

I hope that we don't have to scatter his ashes in the fountain like we did in Geneva. It would be pity to mess up this beautiful place, she thought.

In the elevator on the way to their room Anna asked the princess, "Is this really a seven star hotel?"

"No, my dear it's officially five stars but the service and ambiance is impeccable so it's regarded as being in a league of its own."

With so much gold and vibrant colors everywhere

it was indeed different from other places Anna had seen.

The elevator stopped on 10th floor where their private butler was awaiting them.

"Sajan! How are you? So good to see you again," the princess looked delighted to see him. "How have you been after all this time?"

Sajan, a handsome man in his 30s had the most beautiful smile that exuded warmth and positive energy you could instantly feel.

"May I introduce you to my niece Anna, and this is Sajan, my favorite person in this hotel. I especially asked for him to be here when I made my reservation."

"Your suite is ready for you princess, please follow me."

They went to the right of the open atrium, almost all the way to the end where room 1010 was located. Though 10th floor is not very high compared to the highest 28th floor in the hotel, Anna felt a bit queasy when looking over the side barrier. I'm not good with heights she thought. And the floors here were double, meaning that the 10th floor was in reality the 20th. After all, the hotel is known for being one of the tallest in the world.

The two-story, two-bedroom suite was breathtaking. Sajan showed Anna around.

"Here to the right is the guest toilet," he opened the door to a spacious room with marbled walls. "Here is the office area with the computer and here behind you is the mini bar and the coffee machine."

If front of them was a large salon with breathtaking views of the coast line, the Palm and the

Atlantis on the horizon. To her right, through the floor to ceiling windows, were golden orange and pink swirls streaking a blue sky as the sun set over the pool deck below.

"We just opened the new pool area with two large swimming pools. You can see the salt water infinity pool there," he pointed at it. "There is also another one with fresh water that's not visible from here. You know, all this deck was built in Finland and transported here by ship in several sections. They assembled it here on site."

"How interesting," the princess said. "My Leopold would have loved to see this."

They moved toward the second salon with its sitting area and dining table set for 12. Behind the table was a kitchen. This place is bigger than a house, Anna thought.

"Are all rooms this big in the hotel," she asked Sajan.

"No, this is the two bedroom suite. The regular rooms have one bedroom upstairs and one living room below. Here you have two living rooms and two bedrooms upstairs so it's much bigger than the others. We also have two royal suites on the 25th floor. And of course the Talise spa on 18th floor that you have to visit. You can have a massage there and they have two large indoor swimming pools. From the balcony in the spa you can look down to the lobby below. It's a nice spot to take pictures."

"No thank you, it's already high enough for me here on the 10th floor," she said with a smile.

They continued upstairs to see the bedrooms. On the left was the master bedroom of the princess and on the right the smaller one for Anna. Both rooms had spacious bathrooms with a Jacuzzi bath and separate showers. Anna spotted a full size Jour d'Hermès perfume on the bathroom sink. Can't wait to try it, she thought.

"Oh! I almost forgot, we also have a new bar on the 27th floor. It's called Gold on 27. You must see it. Everything inside there is gold-plated."

"Thank you Sajan," the princess said. "Can you make a reservation for dinner at the Al Mahara restaurant at eight thirty, please? I want to show Anna the aquarium." Then she turned to Anna. "Before we go to dinner let's have a drink in the new golden bar. I want to show you the view and explain something."

They changed to evening dresses and made their way to the 27th floor. Surrounded by gold and glitter the two women settled down next to the window and ordered two glasses of Dom Pérignon, the princess' favorite drink. Anna admired the spectacular view of the city when the princess said, "Do you see the hotel on the beach there below in the shape of a wave? It's the Jumeirah beach hotel. Leopold spent hours sitting on the balcony of that hotel, watching the Burj being built. I would watch the sunset and he would study how they put up the white sail on the front facade, the one that covers the atrium. He was fascinated by the construction work. The entire two weeks we were here he would stare at the building so when the hotel opened in December, 1999 we were the first guests to check in. Before he died, he told me that he wanted part of his ashes to be scattered over the hotel, the front side here with the white sail." She paused and looked at Anna to see her reaction. "The problem is that there are no windows in the hotel that you can open. He didn't think of that."

Anna looked around her only to see floor to ceiling windows, same setup as in their suite.

"Are you sure there are no regular windows in the hotel that can be opened? And what about the roof? Can we get there?"

"We could try. I know there's a helipad on top of the sail. Ten years ago Roger Federer and Andre Agassi were playing tennis there. You must have seen the pictures on the news? It was some kind of a publicity stunt. Anyhow, we could try to get up there but I have acrophobia, fear of heights, so I can't do it."

Anna thought about her own fears, like crossing the high bridge in Gothenburg twice per day. That was scary enough but this hotel is at least two times higher than the bridge.

"I think that I have what you have, I'm scared of heights too. Let me check out this place on my phone. There must be pictures of the roof and the helipad," she said. "According to Wikipedia the helipad is 210 meters high over the sea level. Look at the pictures here. There is a courtyard and metal stairs leading up to the helipad."

The princess had a look at the photos then turned and faced the sky. "Sorry my dear Leopold, we can't do this for you. How about scattering your ashes over the sea instead. Would that work?"

"Wait a minute, I have an idea." Anna just saw a picture of a helicopter with a sign *Helicopter Dubai*

Scenic Tours next to it. "I wanted to see the city and here they have a helicopter tour. If I take it myself, you can sit on the beach and watch me scattering the ashes out of the helicopter's window. Look at the picture here, the helicopter has a window that you can open. How about that?" She was pleased with herself for inventing this fantastic scheme.

"It sounds like a great plan but how will you get to the helicopter without getting dizzy?"

"Good question, let me think about it over dinner."

Sajan was seated at his desk when the women arrived back from dinner. "Welcome back," he said, "how was your evening?"

"Very nice, thank you," said the princess. "We need your help with tomorrow's reservation Sajan. Could you please arrange a helicopter tour of the city for my niece? Around three o'clock in the afternoon? They can pick her up at the roof top, show her the city and the coast line and then land on the Palm to show her the Atlantis hotel. From there she can continue the tour by a private car with a tour guide."

The helipad next to Atlantis hotel was on the ground. This way Anna needed to be on Burj's high helipad only once. It was the best solution they could come up with during the dinner.

"Yes, of course, let me call them straight away. For one person only? Is that correct?"

He talked on the phone for a couple of minutes to confirm the reservation.

"Will you be here tomorrow afternoon?" Anna asked. She had an idea. She would ask Sajan to accompany her to the roof of the hotel and lead her to the helicopter so she could close her eyes until she was inside.

"Yes, I will be here. Call me if you need anything, I'm at your disposal."

He followed them to the end of the corridor and opened the door to their suite.

"Good night ladies, sleep well."

Anna woke up well rested. They have comfortable beds here, I must check where they are coming from, she thought. She lifted up the cotton bed sheets and saw the Swedish manufacturer DUX logo on the mattresses. Really? All the way from Sweden? No wonder I slept this good.

Suddenly her phone rang. It was Elin.

"Can you talk now? It's urgent."

"Why are you whispering?" Anna asked.

"Because I'm in the bathroom and Stefan's wife is sitting on the sofa in the living room. I'm freaking out here!"

"What? Why is she there? Why did you let her in?"

"I didn't. She had her own key. She just unlocked the door and came in when I was sleeping."

"What does she want? What did she say to you?"

"She wants me to move out, right now this minute. She says that the apartment belongs to her company and that I shouldn't be here. She showed me some legal paper and told me to call her lawyer if I didn't believe her. Oh, and there is a guy at the door changing the locks."

"Did you try to call Stefan?"

"Yes, of course but he doesn't answer. I texted him a million times as well. What shall I do now?"

"Can you call the police? She can't throw you out like that. You have been living there for over a year now." Anna wasn't sure what else Elin could do in a situation like this. "If you need a place to stay you can always crash on my sofa, no problem."

"Yeah, I know but I have so much stuff here, all my clothes and shoes and other things. It's impossible to take it all."

"Did you tell her?"

"Yes and she said to pack a bag right now and the rest she will ship to me by tomorrow. She is very persistent you know."

Oh boy, this was a disaster waiting to happen. And where was Stefan now? He was probably hiding somewhere in Stockholm, letting Elin take the heat. His wife must have found out about them and got pissed, Anna thought.

"Listen, my aunt has a spare key to my apartment. I will call her so you can go and pick it up. I should be back home in a few days."

"You are the best," Elin was grateful for having such a good friend in Anna. "Hurry back home, I'm missing you like crazy."

"Yeah, I'm missing you too. You will not believe what I have done these past few days."

"I can't wait to see you so you can tell me all about it. Have to go now, she is knocking on the door," Elin said, her voice shaking.

"Okay, take care and text me later so I know that you are fine."

This was not good. Poor Elin, what will she do now? She had been accustomed to a life in luxury so going back to ordinary living will not be easy for her. On the other hand, being a rich man's mistress isn't really a life goal, is it? Elin could do so much better. She is beautiful and smart, and has great potential to succeed in life on her own, Anna thought. She always knew that Stefan was a schmuck, let's hope this was the end of him.

After breakfast, the princess and Anna went to the swimming pool. As she lay down on her sun bed or swam in the infinity pool, Anna spent hours studying the hotel's structure, thinking about the task that lay ahead of her. What an interesting construction, she thought. On the outside of the building, facing the pool area, she could see people riding in the glass elevators. Wow, that's scary, she thought. This hotel is really high. I don't know if I can do it.

At three o'clock sharp, Anna and Sajan walked up the stairs to the helipad. The chopper was already there waiting for her, it's engine off, so it wouldn't be too windy for them during the short walk to reach it. On the top step she closed her eyes, not daring to look at the view. A gust of wind hit her face, throwing her off balance, so she grabbed his arm for support and with trembling legs moved forward to the helicopter.

Down on the private beach opposite the hotel, the princess took her seat at the bar, ordering a glass of champagne to bid farewell to Leopold. She had a perfect view of the hotel with its helipad on top of the white sailed wall. From her position she couldn't see the chopper, only one of its rotor blades.

The pilot opened the door and helped Anna

inside. "You can open your eyes now miss. You will be fine. Put on your seatbelt here."

The moment she opened her eyes she panicked. Oh my God, this isn't the chopper from the picture I saw yesterday. This one doesn't have a window that you can open. What shall I do now? Think fast! The princess will be hugely disappointed if I screw this up. She might even get a heart attack!

"Excuse me," she said to the pilot who was already in his seat in front of her. "I need to check something quickly. I think that I dropped something. Just give me a second."

She took out the zip lock from her handbag, opened the door and jumped down on the helipad holding tight to the chopper's side. Pretending to look under it, she emptied the ashes on the floor and quickly jumped up again, her heart pounding.

"Can we please go now?" she shouted to the pilot.

Down at the beach the princess had her eyes fixed on the helipad up in the sky. At first she saw the rotor blades moving slowly, then they took up speed and the helicopter lifted up, and forward towards the beach. Suddenly, she saw a cloud of dust lifting up from the helipad to slowly fall down over the white sail. At that moment she burst into tears.

13

GOTHENBURG, SWEDEN

Anna opened the door to her apartment and
gasped in disbelief. For a moment she thought that
she walked into a warehouse. There were boxes
everywhere lined up against the walls, all the way
from the floor to the ceiling. No way! This is not
happening!

Elin was in the kitchen preparing dinner.

"Finally you are back! I missed you so much!"
Elin hugged Anna, both girls jumping up and down.

"Don't worry about the boxes," Elin said. "I'm
looking for an apartment and also for a job. I will be
out of here in no time."

"Sure, you can stay as long as you want, no
problem." Having Elin here was not a problem but
her boxes, that was another issue, Anna thought.

"Come to eat and tell me everything what
happened and I mean *everything*!"

"Sure, where shall I begin?"

A few weeks went by and Elin was still at Anna's. She didn't manage to find work, neither an apartment that she liked.

Meanwhile, Anna kept in touch with the princess making sure the lady was doing fine. Though they had many laughs remembering their antics, Anna could sense that the princess was looking forward to meeting Leopold again, in her own words so to say. One morning Anna received a phone call from Rosita.

"The princess died in her sleep this morning," the maid said sobbing. "You must come to the funeral. I will let you know when."

"Oh no!" Anna cried. Why is this happening to me? What are the odds of three family members passing away within six months? How is this even possible?

She desperately wanted to go to the funeral. When Rosita texted Anna about the details, she booked a ticket and flew in for a day. Luckily, this day was her day off from work.

14

GENEVA, SWITZERLAND

Anna arrived at the church just on time. This place was much smaller than Henri's grand funeral, she noticed. There was a group of 20 to 30 people in front of the altar, none of whom Anna had seen before. She was afraid to meet Maxence again. Fortunately for her he was nowhere to be seen.

She made her way to the front row to spot a crying Rosita holding Coco in her Chanel bag. They hugged and sat down as the organ music started.

Seeing the princess in her coffin in front of the altar broke her heart. So many memories, Anna thought, she was truly a remarkable lady. I will miss her forever. Then she remembered the talk she and the princess had in Monaco, the one about dying people.

"No one ever dies. Their body might be dead but their energy is still here with us," the princess had told her then.

Anna looked around the church hoping to find a

sign from the princess but couldn't see any. She took a deep breath and closed her eyes. A notion of peace came over her. *Everything will be fine. You are fine.*

After the service, princess Sobieski's lawyer went over to Anna and announced an important meeting that she needed to attend next morning. She told him she couldn't because she was flying back to Sweden the same evening but he insisted, stressing to her how important it was that she stayed another day.

Next morning Anna was seated in Maître Haville's office. His secretary brought her coffee and announced that he was running five minutes late. Anna was not happy to be summoned here. Last time she saw the lawyer, in the very same room, he told her that her father didn't include her in his will. She would have to sue his estate, meaning his son Maxence and her father's widow Mathilda to get any money. This lengthy process could take years and cost many thousands Swiss francs, money that Anna didn't have.

The office was located in the old city of Geneva, close to the Russian church with the beautiful golden domes. It looked like a museum with wooden panels on the walls and large paintings framed in gilded ornate frames. The ceiling was carved in wood, something that she had never seen in Sweden. In front of her was a heavy Louis XV desk and an antique chair. Behind the desk, a shelf wall of old thick books with leather covers, embossed with golden letters. The other three chairs in the room were also antique. They were clad in brown leather.

On the floor there was a large dark red Persian silk carpet. The place had an old smell to it, like the time has stood still for the past hundred years.

There was a faint knock on the door. Maître Haville's secretary entered the room with a man and a woman. They were both wearing gray suits. Anna was introduced to them and told they were both lawyers representing the city of Geneva. Shortly after, Maître Haville arrived carrying a heavy folder. He greeted Anna and took his place behind the desk.

"Thank you for coming on such a short notice," he said to Anna. "How are you feeling today?"

"Fine, thank you," she answered shortly. Let's get this over with, she thought.

"The meeting here today is very important to you Miss Andersson so I would advise you to listen carefully and not to speak until you are certain what you are going to say. Do you understand?" he said in a serious tone. Anna was taken aback by this. The other two lawyers in the room looked like they were attending a funeral. What is going on here? she thought.

"I am going to ask you a few questions so please take your time before you answer. Everything will be recorded by the microphone here. Is that okay with you?"

Do I have a choice? she thought. "Yes," she said.

"This is quite an unusual situation that we have here today and therefore I must follow the instructions carefully." He looked at Anna and then at the papers in front of him. The other lawyers in the room opened their folders, ready to take notes.

"Is your name Anna Andersson?"

"Yes, it is," she said, feeling like she was taking part in a police interrogation.

"Do you know Coco, the beige female Chihuahua, princess Sobieski's little dog?"

"Yes, I do," Anna replied without any hesitation.

"Do you like her?"

"Yes, I do," she repeated.

"Would you like to take care of the dog until she dies?" he asked, looking up at her.

"Yes, of course, I would love to but why me and not Rosita, the maid?" she added.

"Because Rosita will be moving back to Spain. The princess bought her a house there so she can live close to her family. The princess wanted Coco to stay in Geneva, a place that she is used to."

"Oh, this could be a problem," Anna replied. "As I can't afford to live here, at least right now. What a shame as I truly like Coco, she is lovely."

The other two lawyers exchanged glances in amusement but said nothing.

"Well, the thing is that Coco comes with the accommodations. Not only the apartment in Geneva but the chalet in Gstaad, the apartments in Monaco, Paris and New York, plus the house in London. Coco is accustomed to all these places."

Anna was not sure if she understood this correctly. If she promised to look after Coco she would be able to use all the houses of the princess? And what about the staff? These places cost a fortune to maintain. Her brain was buzzing.

"Can you please clarify to me what just happened here?" she said looking at Maître Haville, her pulse rising by the minute.

"Princess Sobieski left everything she owned to you Miss Andersson, under the condition that you take care of her dog. Which you agreed to do before you heard about the money involved."

"There is money as well?" Anna asked in disbelief. The princess had been very generous to her already so she didn't expect anything more.

"Yes, there is money, a lot of it, but there is a condition tied to it."

"What is it?" Anna asked.

"The condition is that half of the money has to go to a charity of your choice Miss Andersson. You will have to register a charity foundation with the city of Geneva. The lawyers present here have all the necessary documents for you to sign. You can also employ an assistant to help you cope with the responsibility. The princess suggested someone called Miss Elin. Do you know her?"

"Yes, I do," she said smiling wide. Elin will love this, she thought. "So how much money are we talking about?"

"That is difficult to say because most of it is invested. The princess had a large portfolio so the lawyers are still going through the books. Is that correct?" he asked looking at the gray suits in front of him.

"Yes, we are still working on it," the woman answered. "However, the rough estimate is around 500 million Swiss francs. Plus the real estate. Plus the jewels and art pieces. Plus some more items on the list. There is also the possibility that other relatives of the princess might come forward to contest her will. You have to wait six months before everything is yours. In the meantime you can use the houses and her bank account, as long as you take care of Coco."

"And what will happen when Coco dies?" Anna was not sure how long Chihuahuas live, but for certain it would be less than 15 years. Coco was eight now.

"When the dog dies, everything goes to you and the charity, just like now, no difference," the man in gray suit said in broken English. "And by the way, just to inform you, there is no inheritance tax in Geneva."

Suddenly Anna couldn't breathe.

"Can I open the window please? I need some fresh air."

Maître Haville opened the window behind her.

"Why don't we take a short break?" he said.

When the suits left his office he looked at Anna and said, "There is one more thing the princess wanted you to do."

"What is it?"

"She wanted you to scatter her ashes at the same places as her husband's. She said that you'd know where that would be."

"Yes, I know," she said with a smile, remembering the trip warmly.

"Oh, and she said something about Fiji. She wanted you to go there," he added.

My dear princess remembered, how sweet of her. A feeling of nostalgia swept over Anna. Fidji, her mother's favorite perfume, a beautiful bouquet of rose and jasmine filled her nostrils. She could still smell the powdery floral scent, reminding her of her childhood.

"So now you will have the money to go after the Dupontes. Let me know when you want to start the proceedings."

Anna left Maître Haville's office carrying a briefcase full of documents. I will have to translate everything to Swedish, she thought. This is such a big responsibility. She was grateful and honored to be chosen by the princess. I will not let her down, she thought. There are so many people who need help today; single mothers, women's shelters, animal shelters, cancer research.... Her mind was busy all the way back to the princess' apartment.

Rosita opened the door and then her arms to give Anna a warm welcoming hug. Coco came forward to greet her as well, her little tail wagging frantically as Anna picked her up.

"I love you Coco," she said, kissing her on the head. Coco licked Anna's face, happy to see her.

The End

ABOUT THE AUTHOR

Dr. Bea M. Jaffrey is an American-trained clinical psychologist and psychotherapist in Geneva, Switzerland. She is also a wife and a mother of six children and six Chihuahuas.

Other books by this author:

English

159 Mistakes Couples Make In The Bedroom

And How To Avoid Them

French

159 Erreurs Faites Par Les Couples

Dans La Chambre À Coucher

Et Comment Les Éviter

Spanish

159 Errores De Las Parejas En La Cama

Y Cómo Evitarlos

Italian

159 Errori Che Le Coppie Commettono A Letto

E Come Evitarli

German

159 Fehler Die Paare Im Schlafzimmer Machen

Und Wie Man Sie Vermeidet

77740209R00092

Made in the USA
Lexington, KY
03 January 2018